THE F-WORD

SANDRA MARTON

First Print Edition

ISBN 9780997291551

Published by Sandra Marton

www.sandramarton.com

Published in the Untied States of America

1

So let's get this straight.

This is a story about romance.

Well, it's not a story. I mean, it's not something somebody made up. It's about me. And yeah, in case you're wondering, I'm a guy.

Surprised? Sure you are. You figure those words just don't go together. Romance, with a capital R. Guy, with a capital G. You're probably sitting there and smirking. What could a dude possibly know about romance? You figure we're big on sex. But romance?

You're right.

Romance is not a male thing.

And that's exactly my problem.

The bottom line is that whatever you think you know about men and romance is pretty much correct. You figure we're big on the F-word as long as it stands for Fuck and not Forever.

And we are.

Sure, some of us fall off the cliff once in a while.

Guys get engaged. They get married. If it works, good for them. Just leave the rest of us alone, okay?

We like life precisely the way we're living it. Unencumbered. Nobody to answer to. Work hard, play hard. Drive fast cars or do whatever it is that turns you on, lie around on fall and winter Sundays unshaven, a box of take-out pizza and a six pack of beer not more than a few inches away, and watch football until your eyes glaze over.

And have sex.

Lots of sex.

Slow sex. Fast sex. Sex in five star hotel rooms. Got to say, there's something special about banging a woman against a glass wall overlooking Manhattan. Or in the corner of a museum where somebody might walk by at any minute. Nothing wrong with beds, either. Big beds, with lots of room for action.

Sex is always fine.

Men like doing it, thinking about it, talking about it. Using all those four letter words to describe female parts and the male parts that go with them. And you're already yawning because you figure that's what this is about and, really, how many different ways can there be to describe—sorry, ladies—your basic fuck?

Okay.

But you're wrong.

One, that's not what this is about.

Two, I don't believe in basic fucks. Each time is different. Not just positions. Fucking—sex, if you prefer that word—is never the same twice. At least, it shouldn't be. There are endless variables. Where you are. How you're feeling. Are you in the mood for fun? Maybe for something dark and a little dirty? Something accompanied by rose petals and moonlight? Let's put it this way: If the man in your life delivers the same screw job day after day, year after year, I'm sorry for you.

But, as I said before, none of that matters because that stuff doesn't apply to this situation.

See, this confession—I guess you'd call it that—this confession isn't about fucking. Why would it be? As you may have already figured, based on what I said about basics, I'm just fine with fucking. In fact—not to be boastful or anything—I have been told that I'm just about perfect with it. And—again, not to boast, just to be honest—I am never at a loss for having a woman in my bed. Scoring is my thing. Well, scoring and then delivering the best sex possible.

The truth is that dudes can have a good time just jacking off.

Wait.

I don't mean that. Not exactly. Sex is a hell of a lot better with a woman than it is with your hand. What I'm trying to say is that the best part of sex is watching the woman I'm with get turned on. Watching her come. I love that, love knowing I've done that for her.

So now you're rolling your eyes and you're calling me, what? An arrogant SOB? An egomaniac? A jerk?

I'm not any of those things.

I'm really a nice guy. Seriously. The people who work with me, who work for me—they all like me. Strangers have been known to smile at me, even in the subway where nobody smiles at anybody. I get along with little kids—my three-year-old niece adores me, but hey, the feeling is mutual. Dogs tend to wag their tails the minute they see me. Even cats purr when I pet them.

Anyway, my best friend, Cooper Holloway, is into genetics. He's got a doctorate in biology and he says none of this is my doing. He says it's in my DNA and I shouldn't feel so good about women finding me so, you know, fuckable.

He's also got the irritating habit of reminding me that that he does as well with the ladies as I do. He says it's his charm, good looks, and intelligence—but that it my case, it's strictly my looks.

In other words, I have my chromosomes to thank.

See, for starters I'm tall. Six feet three, and that's without wearing my old, trusty roper boots. No, I'm not a cowboy. I just like roper boots. They work if I'm riding my Harley or driving the classic 'Vette that I restored, and they're perfect if I have to pop onto a job site.

Where was I?

Chromosomes. Right. Well, mine gave me dark hair, kind of an inky black color. Blue eyes. Fairly regular features. And for the past couple of years I've had what my Mom calls facial fuzz.

I also have this series of tattoos on my left arm and shoulder. Got them done years ago, in Kathmandu. Women seem to find them a turn-on, but I didn't get them for that reason...

More about that later.

Did I mention I'm in construction? And design. O'Malley Design and Construction. That's me. Maybe you've heard of us. If you live in the New York City suburbs, it's a good bet that you have...

Where was I?

We were talking about genetics. DNA. The fact that I'm not bad looking.

Okay. I'm good looking.

The guy who stopped me on the corner of Madison and 47th last month said I reminded him of Liam Hemsworth and was I interested in a new career.

This made for two problems.

The first was that I almost killed the poor bastard.

I grabbed him by his necktie and hauled him to his toes before he could choke out that he wasn't hitting on me. He was an agent for a modeling agency. Yeah, I know. Gay pride. The Rainbow Coalition. I'm all for everybody's civil rights, including my right to be a heterosexual male.

The second problem was that after I'd dusted him off, attempted to straighten his tie and said thanks but no thanks to the idea of becoming a male model, I had to pop into the Starbucks up the block, take out my iPhone and check to see who Liam Hemsworth is.

An actor, it turns out. An Aussie. And, okay, I can see the similarities. We're both tall, blue-eyed, square-jawed. Hemsworth looks as if he works out. I don't, unless you call running or playing soccer on Sundays in Central Park or occasionally swinging a hammer or loading pallets at one of my construction sites a workout.

I kind of like to keep my hand in, so to speak.

And my hair's darker than this Liam guy, but you get the picture.

I look okay.

And—do you hear me knocking on wood? And I have a good life.

Nice family, starting with my mom and dad. He's a retired contractor. He owned his own business—small, not big, but he had a rep for being the guy you wanted if you wanted a job done right. I worked for him summers from the time I was fourteen straight through college.

Well, almost straight through.

The summer I graduated from high school, I didn't work for him.

More about that later. Maybe.

Because, you know, this isn't a trip down memory lane. I'm just trying to give you some background here so you can understand how I got myself into this situation.

Mom's an English teacher. She's retired too, but you say something dumb like *him and me* and she'll look you straight in the eye and tell you it's *he and I*. When I was in my teens and she did that to my buddies, even though she did it nicely, I wanted to crawl away and die. Here's the best way to tell you what kind of mom she is—she figured out that those polite corrections just about killed me and she stopped doing it. At least, she let me think she'd stopped doing it. Years later, friends admitted she'd wait until she was alone with whatever kid had just tried to murder the English language and she'd gently offer the correction, and you know what?

They all said they'd been grateful.

I have a sister. Casey. She's two years older than I am—you didn't really think I'd say she was two years older than *me*, did you? We hated each other through elementary school, middle school and part of high school. Then I turned sixteen and she turned eighteen and we looked at each other and saw two human beings instead of two siblings, and we've been close ever since. She's married now, to a terrific guy, and I already mentioned the little niece who owns my heart...

See?

No joke. I really am a nice guy. And okay looking.

Fuckable—although the F word that's turned out to be my problem is a very different one.

It's Forever.

Which is what this is all about.

Yes, I have a serious problem. Or, at least, I had a serious problem. And yes, I walked straight into it because I am what I just said. A nice guy. And because there are people out there who think the Answer to Everything is Finding the Right One.

Your Forever Person.

Crap.

I'm confusing you. I'm confusing myself. So let me back up and start from the beginning. Let me start from when I walked into my office at eight in the morning a few weeks ago...

2

My office, a sprawling glass-and-cedar structure on a couple of acres of woods and meadows, is located just outside New York City in a town called Bedford. I designed the building and the grounds it stands on and, of course, my company built it. It's a great-looking property and I'm lucky to have a great staff, starting with my PA, Bailey Abrams.

Bailey snags me as I step through the door.

"There's a problem at the Schecter site," she says.

I roll my eyes. "And a happy good morning to you, too."

Bailey doesn't even blink and she doesn't slow her pace as she trots alongside me to my office. I have long legs and a long stride, and generally I have to slow down so a woman can keep up with me, even the tallest ones, because they wear those short, tight little dresses and those ridiculous nosebleed heels.

Trust me.

In a national election, I'd vote for both.

But this is my office, where practicality counts. And Bailey is practical. She's down-to-earth. She's not into how she looks. She wears suits and sneakers. The sneakers make it easy for her to cover enough ground to match my pace, and the skirts of those suits are what women call A-shaped. A-line. Whatever. You know what I mean. They're full enough so she can move fast and they're dark in color, probably because that's also practical when she's always rushing around bringing me my coffee—not that I ask her to do that. I mean, I'm an equal op kind of dude. No sexism here, but Bailey thinks keeping me caffeinated is in her job description. Plus she's always handling chalk, scratching my schedule on a chalkboard because I like to be able to look up and see it, cross out stuff, add stuff...

The point is, Bailey is just what I need.

She's been with me from my Wall Street days. Did I mention Wall Street? I guess I should have. I started there with a degree in finance straight out of New York University. Yeah, NYU, where I studied finance on a full scholarship.

Fooled you, right? You thought you had me all figured out. First you pegged me as some rich guy from a wealthy family, and I bet you pictured me spending my college years partying, skiing, living life in the fast lane. Then you decided I was a jock and I'd gone to some big Midwestern university on an athletic scholarship.

Wrong.

I'm rich, but I made all my money myself.

I did my share of partying when I was in college—doesn't everybody? But not anymore.

As for skiing—Yeah. I ski every chance I get. I'm into sports, not just as an observer but as a doer. I was Jerome High School's quarterback; I played midfield on Jerome's soccer team. I ran, I swam, I surfed—bet you didn't know we surf here on the East coast—and I still love all that stuff, but I also have a functional brain. That's what got me into NYU on a full scholarship and into a high-profile job with a hedge fund called Hinchley-Finch.

I stayed with them for three years.

Three endless, agonizing years because it took me that long to finally figure out that no matter how much money I made—and, trust me, I made lots—I was never going to be happy managing the portfolios of rich dudes who drank fifty-year-old Scotch in the evenings and played endless rounds of golf on the weekends.

Three years in, I took a deep breath, quit my job, went back to school for some courses in architectural design and opened O'Malley Design and Construction.

Of course, I'm glossing over the scary spots.

Like cashing in what I'd invested in stocks in those three years. It was—to me, anyway—a small fortune, but I needed the money to buy two incredibly expensive acres of land in Rye—that's an upscale town outside New York City—and put up a four bedroom, five bathroom contemporary complete with gardens and an infinity pool, all on spec. Spec is shorthand for sinking money into a house nobody's asked you to build, meaning you put it up, cross your fingers and hope like hell somebody's gonna come along and fall in love with the place because if nobody does...

But someone did. And that's how I started O'Malley Design and Construction.

With those first bucks safely in the bank, I drew up plans for my headquarters building—and phoned Bailey, who had been my PA at Hinchley-Finch.

"I need a personal assistant," I told her, and before I had the chance to finish explaining my new life and the fact that, for now, I could only afford to pay her half what she was worth, she interrupted and said yes, fine, she'd take the job.

And she's perfect for it. She's organized. Smart. Dedicated. Even better, she doesn't find me intimidating—some people do. She doesn't, you know, drool over me either. She doesn't see me as a guy. And I don't see her as a woman.

I'm getting myself sidetracked here.

Why was Bailey exactly what I needed? Because she's a levelheaded, work-oriented person. We have an excellent relationship. She's a nice girl, she's bright and quick, and—let me get this out of the way even if it's gonna tick off some of you—she's not any kind of distraction for me. How could she be? She's not tall and stacked; she's petite and, well, let's just say she's not at all sexy—and I mean that in the best possible way.

She's definitely not my type of woman, but she's definitely my type of PA.

She has a degree in business from Columbia; she's a model of efficiency; she's always the center of calm in what can often be a frazzled world, and she's completely dedicated to O'Malley Design and Construction.

She is, well, she's Bailey. What more could a man want? And—a quick side-note here—I can now pay her what she's worth to me, which is about four times what she earned on Wall Street.

Bottom line: we're both happy.

We reach the door to my office. I open it and step inside.

Bailey's right on my heels.

"The Schecter problem," she says.

I sigh. "What is it?"

"Bob Emanuel ate some bad clams."

I look at her. Bob Emanuel is the chief carpenter on a job we're doing. Four acres. Low slung house. Eight bedrooms. Nine baths. A Zen garden. A pool with a waterfall. A pool house with an attached yoga room. The place is a blend of Asian and contemporary. It's gonna be spectacular.

"And?"

"And, he spent the night puking up his guts."

I take off my suit jacket. Bailey takes it from me, the way she always does, whisks it onto a hanger, opens the closet door, puts the hanger on the rod, gives the jacket a quick workover with a brush—did I mention I have a dog? A one hundred and fifty pound mastiff that sheds almost that much fur every day.

Bailey hangs the jacket in the closet.

Efficient. Always.

I sit down at my desk. My mug of coffee, black, two sugars, is positioned just where it always is.

I take a sip.

"And I need to know this happy detail because...?"

"Because he's the teak guy."

"The what?"

"The teak..."

Bing bing bing.

Bailey looks shocked. Actually, I'm shocked, too. It's her smartphone. The only other time her phone rang while she was with me was two years back, when her mother called to say her dad was in the hospital.

I look at her.

No. She doesn't look shocked. Or worried. Just... I'm not sure. Annoyed? Upset? Something.

I wave my hand. "Take the call."

"It's a text. And it can wait."

"Don't be ridiculous. See what it is. I hope it's not bad news."

She yanks the phone from her pocket. Looks at it. Then she looks at me. She shakes her head.

"I'll deal with it later."

"Don't be silly. Deal with it now."

"Later," she says firmly. She hits the button that turns off the phone, then jams it back in her pocket. "We were talking about the teak doors."

"The teak doors," I say, but it's difficult to get my head back to the topic. What's going on with Bailey? I can't help but wonder.

She nods. "From Thailand? The ones that date back to the tenth century."

"The temple doors. Of course. What about them?"

"They're due to arrive today and Bob—"

"And Bob's the only guy I want handling them." Shit. I blow out a breath. "Any chance we can hold off delivery for a couple of days?"

"I already called the dock transport people. No way."

Double shit. I trust all my people, but trusting them to deal with doors that set my client back six hundred thousand bucks...

"We must have somebody who knows teak."

Bailey nods. "We do."

"Well, call him."

Bailey looks at me. "Ring-a-ding," she says.

"What?"

"You know teak, Mr. O'Malley."

I stare at my PA. There are two things wrong with her statement.

One, I don't know teak. I mean, not compared to Bob the Barfer. I'm into wood, yeah. I have this thing about looking at a piece of oak or redwood and kind of seeing what form or shape is hiding inside it, but *knowing* teak that's centuries old? Not my specialty.

Two, after all these years, I have yet to convince Bailey to call me Matt. Each time we have this conversation, she tells me she's old-fashioned, that she believes in proper form in the business place, and I tell her that calling the boss *Mister_*went out with typewriters and landline phones.

"I call you Bailey," I invariably say, and she invariably nods and says Yes, that's right, you do. And then she calls me Mr. O'Malley again and I sigh and give up the whole dumb thing for another couple of months...

But right now, that isn't the problem.

She can call me anything she wants except an expert on teak or antiquities, because I am not either.

I tell her that. She shrugs.

"You did that entire teak wall of built-ins in the Genovese house," she says. "Not Bob."

"Yeah, well, that was different. It was a wall, and the teak wasn't older than the hills behind the Schecter place."

"Neither are these temple doors."

This is the kind of answer you get when you deal with a logical person. I shove back my chair and rise to my feet.

"You know what I mean."

"And you chose these doors yourself. You went all the way to Bangkok to see them and make sure they were really what you wanted."

"Who else was gonna do it?"

"And you texted me and told me to tell Mr. and Mrs. Schecter that the doors really were genuine temple doors from the fifteenth century."

"You think that makes me an expert? What it makes me is a guy who read a couple of books before I saw those doors."

Bailey folds her arms over her chest. I say *chest* because I don't think she has breasts under those suit jackets. Not that I spend time thinking about it. Man, what am I talking about? What I mean is, she's flat chested. The suit jackets all hang straight from the top button to the bottom one...and, hell, what has that to do with anything except to remind me that I'm arguing with a woman who graduated Magna cum Laude and who is rarely, okay, maybe never wrong when it comes to knowing what's best for O'Malley Design and Construction?

And what was that all about? That text message she didn't want to deal with? That text message at all, when she never gets messages or calls, at least not here?

I sigh.

I should be concentrating on the teak doors.

She's right.

Somebody has to sign for delivery. More than sign. Stuff like this, there's sure to be a shitload of paper-work. Plus, somebody has to supervise the unloading and uncrating of the doors, check them over, install them, and the only somebody in sight for the physical part of all that is me.

So I sigh again and head for my closet, but Bailey beats me to it. She opens the door, reaches in, takes out a pair of jeans, a blue chambray shirt, heavy cotton socks and the roper boots I mentioned earlier. They've been with me, same as she has, since day one.

Added to everything else, the woman reads minds.

"I'll phone for a car."

"No car," I say as I undo my tie. "We'll take one of the trucks."

I toss the tie on the desk. Bailey picks it up,

smooths it out and marches to the closet to hang it over a hook.

"Very well, sir."

If I'm not *Mister*, I'm *sir*. So old-fashioned. So, I don't know, so obedient.

Under other circumstances, meaning, coming out of another woman's mouth at a different time, different place those words—*sir, mister*—might get a reaction from me. Well, from a part of me. The part behind my fly, which is always ready and happy to participate in something new.

"Shall I tell José to stand by?"

"José?" I unbutton my white broadcloth shirt. I'm not into T-shirts so what I'm uncovering is my naked chest. Bailey doesn't so much as blink. Why would she? That's one of the benefits of having a neutral relationship. "Why do we need José?"

"To drive the truck."

"I'll drive it myself."

"Very well, Mr. O'Malley. I'll call and tell the foreman to expect you in half an hour."

"Fine." I yank my shirttails free of my trousers. "And see what you can scrounge up to change into."

This time, she does blink. "Me?"

"You." I undo my cuffs. "I'll deal with the doors. You'll deal with the paperwork."

She nods and turns towards the door. "I'll requisition a pair of coveralls from Supplies."

"And boots."

"Boots. Of course."

She starts for the door again.

"One more thing," I say.

Bailey swings towards me just as I'm peeling off my shirt. There's barely a pause before she turns away again, but not before I see a faint wash of pink spread over her cheeks. Is she blushing? I'm baffled. Then I realize that no shirt isn't the same as an open shirt.

Uh oh. I've embarrassed her.

"Sorry," I say quickly.

"No problem, sir."

Maybe I misunderstood. She certainly doesn't sound embarrassed. And when she turns towards me again, her expression is as professional as always.

"Mr. O'Malley?"

"Yes?"

"You were saying...?"

What *was* I saying? I'm still puzzled by that blush.

"I was saying...Oh. Yeah. Call Burt." Burt's my foreman. "Tell him we're on our way and if the truck delivering the doors arrives before we do, he should just stall them. Then meet me in the lobby. Five minutes."

Bailey nods. "Five minutes."

"Fine," I say, but I don't reach for my belt or anything else until the door shuts firmly behind her.

Okay, I think as I change out of my suit. Okay. Today I get to be a construction guy.

The truth is, even the thought makes me happy.

3

I t takes half an hour to reach the Schecter site.

I consider mentioning that text message, but I don't do it. Bailey's private life is her private life. I don't know anything about her, well, nothing beyond the fact that she has that degree and that she comes from some town in upstate New York. Troy. Schenectady. Something like that.

So we spend the time with her reading me the specifics of the teak temple doors from the dealer's catalogue where I first discovered them, and I try to envision where I'll be placing the necessary screws and fasteners when I install them.

The screws and fasteners, made to order by a place in California, cost three thousand bucks all by themselves so, yeah, this job is a big deal—and actually, I'm looking forward to it. It's been a long time since I did anything meaningful in the field. Too long, I think, as we turn onto a quiet road that leads to the Schecter place.

My guys are happy to see us.

They weren't looking forward to the doors being delivered without Barfing Bob on hand, except they didn't want him there if he was barfing.

They greet Bailey as they always do the times she shows up with me. High fives, hand shakes, nods of the head. They see her as one of them, which is good. The last thing you want on a construction job is some hot babe to distract everybody. Of course, you can't say that, not in today's litigious world, but everybody knows it. Burt put it best the time we'd hired a plumber who also happened to be a babe.

"Got a problem here, boss," he said after she'd been with us a couple of months.

"Which is?" I asked.

I remember Burt looking around, making absolutely sure we were alone. Then he leaned in close enough for me to figure out he hadn't really stopped smoking, the way he claimed.

"The new guy. I mean, the new girl."

"Woman," I said.

"Girl. Woman. The thing is, she's gotta go."

"She's not working out? Her references were—"

"She's a good plumber. She's also female. The guys..."

"If they're coming on to her, Burt, it's your job to stop them."

Burt shook his head. "That's not the problem."

"So what *is* the problem?"

"She drops a wrench, four guys rush over to pick it

up. She starts to lift a box, they trip over each other running to help her. You know what I mean?"

I knew.

My crew was treating the lady plumber like a lady instead of like a plumber.

It was a serious problem. It took me a month to figure out how to ease her out of the job without laying the burden of it on her—and without anybody ending up in court. We did it by transferring her to another site where two of the crew were female and the odds of creating a problem were limited.

Bailey was with me the day we told the plumber we were moving her elsewhere. Afterwards, Burt yanked off his hardhat and swiped an imaginary layer of sweat off his forehead.

"Phew," he said. "Glad that's over. I know I ain't supposed to say it, but women don't belong on jobs with men. Oh, not you, Bailey," he said hastily. "You're never a problem."

I recall thinking that as well meant as the comment was, it might be a little rough, but Bailey took it like the pro she is, just nodded and gave Burt a kind of quick smile as she stood there next to me, all but swallowed up in the coveralls she'd borrowed from Supplies.

She's swallowed up in this current pair, too. She's got the sleeves rolled up. The same for the cuffs. Still, the coveralls look huge on her. The boots, too.

Or maybe it's that she looks small. No. Wrong word. She looks kind of, uh, kind of delicate.

She catches me staring at her.

"Something wrong?"

"Why didn't you take a pair of coveralls that would fit you? " I jerk my head at her ankles. I don't know why, but I sound pissed off. "Those pants roll down, you could trip and fall."

She looks down at herself, then up at me.

"You're worried about accident reports," she says briskly. "No need. I'm not about to trip. Or fall."

"Still," I say, "next time, requisition a size small."

"This *is* a size small," she says.

Dammit, must logic always win?

And that's the end of the conversation.

THE MORNING TURNS out to be fun.

As intended, Bailey deals with the paperwork—it's fucking endless—while I deal with the teak. We unload it. Uncrate it. Check it over, inch by inch. Then we move it—it takes three of my guys plus me. The doors are going to the rear of the house where they'll open onto the Zen garden. Yeah, I know. I'm mixing cultures. Thai temple gates, Japanese garden, but it's all good. It all goes together just fine.

Burt puts the little box of attaching stuff on the floor next to me.

"Here we go," I say.

I look up. Everybody's eyes are on me. Well, no. Not my PA's. Bailey is staring at her smartphone. Is she finally checking out that message? I'm kind of surprised she's doing it at a moment like this and I find myself waiting until she finishes reading, taps in a reply, then just stands there until, obviously, a response comes through. She must have turned off the sound but I can tell she's had a reply because her mouth goes all tight and grim.

I clear my throat.

"Here we go," I say again.

Bailey looks up. Looks around. Damned if she doesn't blush again.

"Sorry," she says, jamming the phone into her pocket.

I take a deep breath and get to work.

To my relief, Bob's done all the prep work exactly right.

The doors fit into the space he prepared as if they'd always hung there. The screws, the special tools he'd ordered...Perfect.

I work slowly. Carefully. It takes me two hours to hang the doors. By the time I'm finished, most of the crew is standing around behind me.

I step back. "Done," I say.

"Fuck," one of the electricians whispers, and that just about sums it up.

The doors are not just spectacular; they look as if they've come home.

There's a faint smattering of applause. For the centuries-old work, not for me, which is just how it should be. Burt produces a case of cold beer. We pop the tops and drink to what's rapidly starting to look like the best project we've done yet—and that's saying something.

We joke, laugh, kibitz for a few minutes. Then the

guys get back to work and Bailey and I head for the truck.

"Those doors," she says as we drive away. "I mean, wow."

I flash her a smile. "Really something, huh?"

She nods. "The Schecters will be happy."

"They'd better be."

We both chuckle.

"They're flying in early next week," I say. "They want to see how things are going."

"Well, they're going to be delighted. Which reminds me. You had a call from that couple, the ones who want a colonial on those hilly four acres in Rye."

"It's the wrong house for the wrong lot. Besides, if they're set on something that traditional, they don't really want me. Give them a call. See if you can set up something for—"

A phone rings. Bailey's. Definitely not mine. Mine plays the opening chords to *Wild Horses*.

Hers plays Beethoven.

"Excuse me," she says politely and she takes the phone out of her pocket, checks the screen and puffs out a little breath of air as she puts the phone to her ear. "Hi, Mom."

I pay attention to the road. For openers, I want to give her some privacy. Plus, the way she said that *Hi, Mom* tells me she's not happy to get this call. I don't know much about Bailey's mother. I don't know much about her family at all. We don't talk about personal stuff, Bailey and I. All I know is what I told you before, that her father is gone.

Come to think of it, she seems a little subdued after weekends home lately. She's been going home more often since her father died, maybe once a month—I only know this because the Fridays she's heading home, she comes to the office with an overnight bag. As for the subdued part—she's kind of quiet on the Mondays afterward. When I ask if she's okay, she always says she's fine, just tired from the travelling. And then I always say she could take a longer weekend, three days, four, and she always says, very politely, "Thank you, Mr. O'Malley, but that isn't necessary."

Now it occurs to me that maybe what she seems those Mondays isn't so much tired or even subdued as, you know, worn down.

"Mom," I hear her whisper, "I already said, I'm not coming. No. I don't care if you told them I'd be there. I am not—"

I take a quick look. Bailey's huddled in the corner and turned as far towards the window as she can get.

She needs more mental space for this conversation.

I reach out, punch in something, anything on Sirius. Shit. The music comes on so loud that we both jump.

Bailey looks at me. I mouth "Sorry," and shut off the sound.

If there were a place to turn off so I could park, get out of the car and leave her alone with the call, I would, but the road we're on is narrow and trees press in on either side

There's some more back and forth, with Bailey's answers coming fast. They're one-word answers. The fact is, all of them are "No," and her voice is rising and rising and then she makes this strangled sound, pounds her fist against her thigh and says, "What do you mean, why? Because I don't want to, that's why! I am not going to cousin Violet's wedding!"

There is a two second pause.

"Is that what you think, Mother? Well, you're wrong. It is not because I'm embarrassed to show up without a date! In fact, I have a date! That's right. A date. A man. A gorgeous, successful, fantastic man. He's taking me away for a weekend of hot sex, not for a weekend at Cousin Violet's fucking wedding!"

I can feel my eyeballs pop.

Did my logical, always calm, always proper PA just drop the F-bomb? Did she say hot sex?

Is she really going away for the weekend with a man?

Apparently, the answers are yes and yes. I don't know abut the weekend part, but telling her mother about the hot sex thing? Saying the F-word? Both happened. And she doesn't just end the call, she slams the phone against the dashboard and then drops it into her lap where it lies as still and silent as a dead mouse.

I am not stupid enough to say a word. Hey, I might be a dude, but even I know when to keep quiet.

Bailey sighs. It's a sad sound, and I look at her. She's looking out the window. In fact, her nose is all but pressed to the glass.

She mumbles something.

"What?"

"I said, I'm sorry."

"For what? You don't owe me an apology."

She doesn't answer. I wait. And wait. I tell myself not to speak...

Myself doesn't listen.

"Bailey?"

"Yes?"

"What's the matter?"

She shoots me a look. I deserve it. What kind of question is that? I know what's the matter. Her mother's nagging her about a party she doesn't want to go to. She wants to spend the weekend with a man instead.

Except, that isn't true.

There is no gorgeous, successful, fantastic man whisking my PA away for the weekend. It's a lie. A protective lie. And yes, it's cruel for me to be as sure of that as I am that the sun rises in the east each morning, but there it is.

There's no studly stud waiting in the wings. There's no guy from GQ hovering. There's no guy, period.

And maybe that's the exact reason Bailey doesn't want to go to the party.

I mean, I remember when Casey was in high school. Eighth grade. We laugh about it now, that eighth grade was not her finest hour. Finest year. You know what I mean. She had braces on her teeth, she was growing so fast that she'd taken to walking so hunched over that I helpfully called her Quasimodo, and a squadron of zits had taken over her forehead.

Of course, by ninth grade she was tall and proud of it; the braces were gone; her skin was flawless. She was gorgeous—she still is—and now we can think back and roll our eyes.

But not then.

I can recall, all too clearly, her flat-out refusal to attend the eighth grade graduation dance, where she was sure she'd be the only girl without a date.

I clear my throat.

"Weddings always suck."

Bailey shoots me a look. "It was impolite to listen to the conversation, Mr. O'Malley."

"I didn't listen. Well, yeah, I did, but only because I couldn't avoid listening. I tried not to, remember? I turned on the radio..."

"It's Cousin Violet who sucks."

Wow. That's the first time I've ever heard my PA say a mean thing about anyone.

"We're the exact same age. Exact! We were born on the same day. Same hospital."

I risk a glance at Bailey. She's sitting with her arms folded, starting straight ahead.

"My whole life, I had to share birthdays with her."

"Well," I say helpfully, "I'm sure it's not fun to know some other person is—"

"Our mothers made one party. One party! For the two of us. And it always was at Violet's house because her house was bigger. Her yard was bigger. Big enough for pony rides, even though I loathed them!"

Silence. Am I supposed to say something here? I shoot another glance at her. Yes. It's my turn, but, shit, what can I...

"Not the ponies," she says. "I loved the ponies. It

was seeing them used like that. You know. Going back and forth, back and forth, kids riding them, yelling, shouting, digging their heels into the ponies' bellies..."

"I think they probably dug their heels into the ponies' flanks," I say, being helpful again.

Bailey gives me a look I deserve. She's feeling pity for the ponies, and I'm correcting her pony parts.

"And there was always cake. Chocolate cake. I *hate* chocolate cake!"

This time, I am smart enough to keep quiet.

"With vanilla frosting. I *hate* vanilla frosting."

There's a sign ahead. The ramp for the highway is coming up. Thank you, God. Once we're on the highway, we'll be back at the office in less than ten minutes.

"Violet always wore lacy dresses. Ruffley dresses. So my mother made me wear them too."

Another bleep of silence. It goes on long enough so I know I have to say something, and not what I'm thinking which is that I don't think ruffley is a word.

"And, uh, and I bet you hated—"

"I did not hate them! I just looked awful in them. Violet was round and plump. I was round and fat."

I open my mouth to tell her that I don't get the distinction, but when I look at her I see that she's looking at me. Glaring at me. As if she's daring me to be dumb enough to say exactly what I was going to say.

I keep silent.

"We were always in the same schools. The same classes."

Okay. I'm sure I'm on steady ground here. I look at Bailey and smile.

"Where you outdid her, right? She got C's. You got A's. You aced every exam. She flunked them all and —Hey!"

Bailey has just slugged me.

It's not much of a slug, just a balled up fist to the arm, but Jesus H. Christ, my calm paragon of efficiency is morphing from Dr. Jekyll to Mr. Hyde.

"She got C's. I got A's. Do you really think that was good, Mr. O'Malley? Do you think having my whole family talk about me being so bright and Violet being the godddamn Queen of the May was a good thing?"

"Queen of the May?"

"It's just a saying. An expression. She was Homecoming Queen. She was Summer Festival Queen." Bailey makes a gulping sound. "She was Winter Festival Queen." Another gulping sound. "And I was an honors student. An honors student! An honors..."

She makes another gulping sound and, holy crap, I realize that she's sobbing.

The on-ramp for the highway is just ahead, and right before it there's a big, wide shoulder. No trees. Just a shoulder. I turn the wheel hard and pull onto it, unbuckle my seat belt, unbuckle Bailey's, and pull her into my arms.

She's not just sobbing. She's flooding us both. My jacket. My shirt. Tears and, man, tears and snot because her nose is leaking.

I lift my ass enough so I can dig into my pocket for my handkerchief. Thankfully, it's unused.

"Here," I say, and I hold the white cotton square to her nose.

Her hand closes over mine and she gives a honking blow.

I go on holding her. It feels awkward. Until this moment the only parts of Bailey I've ever touched are maybe her hand or her elbow or her shoulder, so this really does feel, you know, weird. Not only have I never held her, I've never held anybody wearing coveralls. They're stiff and scratchy, but beneath them is a woman.

I know that sounds ridiculous.

Let me rephrase that.

Beneath them, I can feel that Bailey is a woman.

Jesus. That's even more ridiculous.

What I mean is, of course she's a woman. I always knew that. It's just that she's, you know, female. Soft. Round, in the nicest possible way. Delicate, like I thought before...

She blows her nose again, pushes free of my arms and sits up straight.

"I've made a fool of myself," she says.

"No. No, you have not."

"I have."

"You haven't. Listen, the thing with your cousin Violet? Did you ever figure out a way to get even?"

She looks at me and cocks her head. Her hair has come loose of its rubber band. Her eyes are glittery from her tears. She looks sad and it breaks my heart. She's such a good person. I hate to see her so unhappy.

"How could I? She's always been perfect."

"Really? Seems to me what she's been is perfectly awful."

That wins me a tiny smile.

"Nobody else thinks so," she says. "Only me."

"Baloney. I'm betting half the people who know her hate her. She probably kicks puppies."

Okay. That gets me a watery laugh, but the laugh fades and becomes a sigh.

"The thing is, she'll know."

"Know what?"

"That I won't be, you know, I won't be doing what I told my mother."

"Ah. Going away for a weekend of hot sex with some lucky guy."

She blushes. "Yes."

"How will she know?"

Bailey sighs again. "She just will. They all will. I mean, I'm not...That lie I told my mother. I'm not—I'm not a woman a man would take away for—for—you know, for what you said."

"A weekend of hot sex," I say, and her blush deepens. "Why not?"

"Why not?" She pulls back and stares at me. "I'm the girl who got straight A's. Violet's the girl who got the boys."

"That was a long time ago. Things change."

Another sigh. "Violet will see right through that story about the weekend and—you know—and—"

"A guy who'll want you for hot sex," I say solemnly.

"Yes. There's no way to fool her."

But maybe there is.

A plan is forming in my mind. It's crazy. Anybody would think so. On the other hand...

"Look," I hear myself say, "I have an idea."

"About what?"

"About your cousin's wedding."

"Mr. O'Malley. Thank you for listening to me. But really, I'll get through this. I'll stay home. Or maybe I'll go. I mean, it's just a weekend. I can survive…What?"

"Here's my idea," I say. "Why don't I go with you?"

4

Bailey looks at me as if I've gone nuts. I don't think so. I mean, what have I got to lose?

"Huh?"

"Your mom's never met me. She would have, if I'd gone to your dad's funeral, but I was in Chicago, remember?"

"Mr. O'Malley. I don't know what you think that would accomplish. I mean, it's nice of you to, I don't know, to offer to be there to give me courage, but—"

"This isn't about courage, Bailey. It's about you having a gorgeous, successful, fantastic guy to take you to that wedding."

Her eyes are widening. They're interesting eyes. I always thought they were brown, but they're not. They're damn near black.

"You?"

"Well, yeah." I grin. "I don't know about the gorgeous part. Not the fantastic one, either. But you have to admit, I'm successful." I look down at myself.

My hands are rough looking, a couple of nails a little jagged after two hours spent with those doors, and there's some glue on my jeans. I look up and smile. "I'm a little messy right now, but I clean up pretty good."

"No!" Bailey shakes her head. "What I mean is, thank you. But I couldn't possibly impose..."

"It'll be fun."

"Fun?" She looks at me as if I'm nuts. "Fun? A weekend with my family, with my cousin Violet and her obnoxious, about-to-be husband will be *fun*?"

"Is he really obnoxious?"

"Is the sky blue?"

"And Violet? No redeeming virtues?"

Bailey looks me straight in the eye. "Not a one."

I chuckle. "Think of what a good time we'll have, Bailey, rocking their smug little world."

She stares at me. And stares. She's going to say no, and for some crazy reason, "no" is not what I want to hear.

So I take a breath. Lean forward. I kiss her. Lightly. My mouth brushing over hers. Just brushing. It's a friendly kiss—until she makes a little sound in the back of her throat and I feel her lips cling to mine. Or maybe not. Maybe it's my imagination. It must be, because the entire thing lasts just a couple of seconds, but I feel a kind of thump in my chest, as if something's interfered with my breathing.

Must have been all that working with old wood and glue.

"I know what you're thinking," I say brightly.

She touches the tip of her tongue to the center of her bottom lip.

"You do?"

"Sure. You figure it'll never work. That we won't be able to fool anybody. But we will. We're old friends. I know you know and you know me."

"But we don't," she says. "Know each other. We're not old friends. I'm your assistant. And you're my boss. And we'd be pretending to be, you know, to be—"

Man. Didn't I once see an adults-only movie with that plot?

This is definitely not the time to think about that.

"To be dating," I say briskly. "And of course it would work. We'll look comfortable together."

"We will?"

"Yeah. Because we know stuff about each other. The kind of stuff that, you know, says we're, uh, we're a couple."

Bailey shakes her head. Doubt is written across her face.

I roll my eyes.

"How do I take my coffee?" I ask.

"What?"

"Just answer the question. How do I take my coffee?"

"Black. Two sugars."

"What's my favorite sport?"

"You mean, like you play soccer in Central Park on Sundays? Or that sometimes you watch English rugby on the big flatscreen in your office when you're supposed to be doing paperwork? Or that you drive all the way to Massachusetts for every Patriots home game even though the Giants and the Jets are both New York teams because you think it's wrong that they both actually play in New Jersey?"

I am impressed. I tell Bailey that.

She shrugs, draws a little further away and begins trying to smooth back her hair, which is impossible because it started to rain a while ago and I have the windows of the truck down and it's obvious that Bailey's hair is turning into a mass of curls.

How come I never knew that before? That she has such soft-looking curls?

And how come she's giving me this smug look?

"And what do you know about me?" she says.

"A lot."

"For instance."

I think. I think harder. And I realize that what I know is that she's smart, that she has a degree in business, she has a mom in upstate-wherever-it-is New York. Oh. And she has a nasty cousin named Violet.

Crap.

That's all I have.

"See?" She folds her arms and the smug look grows even more smug. "You don't know a thing about me, Mr. O'Malley. We could never fool my family for an hour, let alone an entire weekend."

An entire weekend? I must have said the words out loud because the smug look disappears and is instantly replaced by one that says forget the whole thing.

"Uh huh. Friday evening through Sunday afternoon. So, thanks for the offer, but—"

"Today is Tuesday."

"So?"

"So, that gives me four days."

"Four days to do what?"

"To get to know you."

"It's more like three days," Bailey says, "and it's impossible."

Logic tells me she's probably right. It tells me that you can't really learn a lot about someone in so short a time. Even if you could, logic also tells me that as much as I love my own family, long weekends spent with family can be, you know, daunting.

On the other hand, I already made an offer. And I'm not a guy who backs down. Added to that, I am into winning. The lady might know how I take my coffee and my sports, but it's evident she doesn't know that other stuff.

I turn away and shift the truck into gear.

"How do *you* take your coffee?" I say.

She heaves an exasperated sigh. "Really, sir—"

"Light? Black? Sugar? Sweet 'N Low?" I pull onto the ramp, check the mirror, step on the gas and merge onto the highway. "Just don't tell me you take it without caffeine."

"I drink tea," she says, "as if it matters."

"What kind? Green? Black? Orange pekoe?" I feel her staring at me and I flash her a grin. "I'm not a complete barbarian," I say. "I know what tea is."

"It's white tea."

"White tea?"

"Yes, Mr. O'Malley. It's picked before the leaves are—"

"That *Mr. O'Malley* thing has to go."

"Really, sir—"

"Same with the *sir* routine." I check the mirror, pick up some speed and pass a line of cars. "Loose." She looks at me. "The tea. Am I right?"

She gives a quick nod.

"Okay. White tea. What else should I know? Sports. Are you into sports?"

Silence. Then she sighs again. "No."

"Not even to watch? Baseball?"

She rolls her eyes.

"Football?"

Another roll of the eyes. "Grown men," she says, "pummeling each other into the dirt."

"Sometimes it's into the mud," I say helpfully. She makes a face. "Okay," I say. "How about hobbies?"

"Not really."

"Meaning?"

"Well, I like to go to go to gallery showings. Museums. I like to walk along the beach. Jones Beach, when I can. That's out on—"

"On Long Island. Great beach. Anything else?"

" I like classical music."

"I knew that," I say triumphantly.

"You did?"

"Of course. Your cell phone. Beethoven's *Fifth*."

"Holsts' *The Planets*."

"Yeah. That's what I meant. Come on. What other things do you like to do?"

"I like to read."

"Ah. Those books with sexy guys on the covers? What are you reading right now?"

"*War and Peace*," she says coolly. "If there's a sexy guy on the cover, I haven't noticed."

War and Peace. It figures.

"What's your idea of a perfect late night snack?"

She doesn't hesitate. "Cereal."

"Cereal?"

"Yes," she says, not just coolly, but defiantly. "I'm sure that isn't your idea of—"

"Cap'n Crunch? Or Frosted Flakes?"

I can feel her staring at me. I look at her and shrug. "We all have our secrets, Bailey. Midnight raids on bowls of crispy stuff smothered in milk happen to be one of mine."

She smiles, but it doesn't last. By the time we pull off at our exit, she's back to shaking her head.

"Thank you for trying, sir, but it wouldn't work."

I turn onto the long driveway that leads to the O'Malley offices and pull up before the front door.

"Even if I wanted to accept your generous offer—"

"It's not generous. It's just one friend helping another."

"We really aren't friends, sir. And that's the point. There's just too much to learn about each other and not enough time to do it. But I thank you for—"

"White tea. Loose, not bags. Tolstoy. Jones Beach. Grown men beating each other up. Which is not what football is, by the way, but you're entitled to your own opinion."

"That's very good, Mr. O'Malley, but—"

"I'm a quick study."

"Perhaps." Her hand is on the door handle. "But my mother is sharp. She'd see through our routine in an instant."

"She would, if you keep calling me Mr. O'Malley."

"Really, Mister..." She stops. Takes a breath. "Look, it's not that I don't appreciate your offer, but—"

"Although, who knows, if anybody hears you addressing me so formally—sir, Mister— they'll figure maybe we have an interesting thing going in the bedroom."

Dumb thing to say, but if I'm going to think of Bailey as, ah, as my woman I have to start talking to her as if we spend our time having fun together instead of working our asses off.

She swings towards me. I can see the color rushing into her face.

Jesus, her hair really is a mess.

I reach out and run my fingers through it. Just to smooth it out. No other reason. Nothing to do with the softness of it, or the way those little curls wind around my fingers.

"But just to be clear, whatever happens in the bedroom would be strictly your choice."

"Nothing will happen in the bedroom," she says, shoving my hand away.

"No. Yes. It was a joke."

"The whole idea is a joke. I am not going to do this ridiculous thing."

I shrug. I sit back, my hands on the steering wheel.

"Have it your way," I say. "Don't go to the wedding. Let your cousin Violet win. Or go to the wedding and let her win anyway. Because whether you're a no-show or you turn up alone, the game will go to her."

I hate myself as soon as the words are out of my mouth. And I don't really mean them. Why would a bright woman like my PA give a crap what her scuzzy-sounding cousin thinks? So why did I say something like that? It couldn't be because I want her to agree to what admittedly is a crazy scheme...

"You're right."

I blink. And look at her. She is staring straight at me, arms folded, chin high.

"I am?"

"She stole my favorite doll when we were six. Did I tell you that?"

"Uh, no. No, you didn't."

"Stole it. And pulled off Suzy's head."

"Suzy?"

"My doll. Violet wasn't happy with just stealing her. She had to kill her." The way she says it, I expect her eyes to blur with tears. Instead, her chin goes up another inch. "I hated her for that. Dammit, I still hate her!"

Another curse word? I'm stunned. But Bailey's not finished yet.

"It's time Violet found out I'm every bit as good as she is."

"Better," I hear myself say.

"Better. Much better." Her eyes narrow. She gives me the kind of look the asp must have given Cleopatra in their last minutes together. "Did I tell you about her fiancé?"

I don't get the chance to answer, because Bailey doesn't give me the chance.

"She says he owns his own business. And he does." The snake-to-Cleo look is gone. It's been replaced by the way I figure a cat looks at a mouse. "He owns three launderettes."

"Well," I say cautiously...

"Washers. Dryers. Detergents." She makes a sound that cannot mean she's a fan of washers, dryers and detergents. "He's an inch shorter than she is even though he wears, what do you call them? Elevator shoes."

A picture swims into my head of a guy standing in an elevator with a box of Tide in his arms.

"And he's pudgy." She gives a little shudder. "I was up for a weekend the start of the summer. Mom had just sold the house and she was moving into a condo... Never mind all that. The point is, Mom gave this Goodbye House, Hello Condo barbecue. Lots of people were there, including, of course, Violet and Chester."

"Chester?"

Can a cat curl its lip while it decides what to do with a mouse?

"Chester. Not even 'Chet.' Everyone calls him Chester." Another shudder. "He walked around shirtless. "

I am getting confused. The woman seated next to me is not a woman I know.

"Shirtless?"

"Yes. At Mom's barbecue. Shirtless. Wearing Bermuda shorts. And lace-up black shoes. With socks."

"Not good," I say carefully.

"I came this close," she says, holding up her hand, thumb and forefinger a hair apart, "*this close* to begging him to put his shirt back on." This time, the shudder is huge. "He's flabby. Like a dead fish. And he's the color of toilet paper."

A dead fish, wrapped in toilet paper. Wearing elevator shoes, and don't forget that box of Tide

Charming.

"So, yes," she says." I accept your offer. You can be my date for the weekend."

I nod. "Thank you," I say. I mean, what else can I say? Somewhere along the line, we've gone from me offering my help to me being grateful she's willing to accept it.

"Seven o'clock," she says.

"Seven o'clock what?"

"I'll meet you back here tonight. At seven. I have to go home first and feed my cat."

"You have a cat?"

Two parallel appear between her eyebrows. I can tell that all that determination is suddenly wavering.

"See? There's so much for you to learn about me—"

"I only meant that I'll have to go home first, too. I have a dog."

"Of course you have a dog. A mastiff. His name is

Walter. He's three years old, his birthday is January 16, and he's up to date on all his shots."

I stare at her. Then it hits me. Bailey has Walter on her schedule. She makes his veterinarian appointments. Heck, she made the arrangements for me to buy him in the first place.

"You're right," I say slowly. "You know everything about me and I don't know a damn thing about you."

She nods. The parallel lines return. Her shoulders slump.

"And I was right about this never working," she says. "We could never pull this—"

"Seven o'clock," I say firmly. "Not here. At your apartment."

"What?"

"We only have three days, Bailey. If we go at this as if we're cramming for finals, it won't work."

"I never crammed for finals."

"I'm sure you didn't, so you'll have to trust me here. Cramming works for facts. What year was the Treaty of Paris signed? How many lanterns were hung in the belfry of the old North church on the night of Paul Revere's ride? What's the meaning of life?"

"Seventeen eighty-three. Two. And there is no specific answer to the last—"

"My point exactly. Some questions can't be dealt with by memorizing facts. If we're going to find out stuff about each other, real stuff, we have to do it by spending time with each other. In suitable settings, so we can really see what we're like away from the office."

She's looking at me as if I'm certifiable. Maybe I

am, but I'm pretty sure what I'm saying makes sense. I want it to make sense, anyway, and I'm not about to try and delve into that. Not right now.

"Okay," I say briskly. I reach across and open her door. My arm brushes lightly over her breasts. Her breath catches. So does mine. Dammit. It's all those fumes from the centuries-old teak. "I'm going to head home. You do the same."

Bailey glances at her watch. "It's only one-thirty."

"Right. Right. Fine. I'll, ah, I'll take a look at that property."

"Which property?"

An excellent question because I came up with that on the spot, but the last thing I want to do right now is spend the next couple of hours in my office.

"The hilly one. The one that couple is thinking of buying so they can put up a colonial."

"It's the wrong house for the site."

I smile. For some crazy reason, I like that she thinks that. "Yeah. I agree." I clear my throat. "Anyway, I'll see you at seven."

"Do you know my address?"

"Of course I know your address."

She looks doubtful. She's right to look doubtful. I don't know her address, but there's always Google.

"Don't cook," I add. "I'll bring dinner."

"I never cook," she says. "I believe in Lean Cuisine."

"And I believe in take-out. See? We've learned something new about each other already."

She gives me a look filled with doubt. Then she

sighs, climbs down from the truck and stands there looking at me through the open door.

"Are you sure you want to do this, sir?"

"Matthew."

I can see her swallow. "Are you sure you want to do this...Matthew?"

A million billion people have said my name in my lifetime. Well, not exactly. I always introduce myself as Matt. I have no idea why I just told Bailey to call me Matthew. I also have no idea why the sound of her saying it made the hair rise on the back of my neck.

"Absolutely," I say.

She nods and shuts the door. I wave. She steps back and I roar off in the traditional cloud of dust, except I don't feel like the Lone Ranger.

I feel like a dude in desperate need of a shrink.

5

I drive around for a while. I take a look at the hilly four acres. I walk it and I know that I was right. It's waiting for a builder who isn't me. I'm into open-plan contemporaries, not colonials. That's why my clients come to me.

These people need a different builder even though I'd love to put a house here. The view is forever, and there's wildlife. Deer. Foxes. Fishers. Birds. The land has everything I'd want if I were buying and building. Which I am not.

I get back into my truck, take out my phone, and send myself a note.

Normally, I'd have texted Bailey. For some reason, the idea of contacting her now makes me, I don't know, uncomfortable. Have I done the right thing? Can we make enough progress to pull off this charade?

More than that, how will it be to spend a long weekend pretending she and I have something going?

What happens the following Monday, when we see

each other in the office? Will it be back to Mr. O'Malley and sir? How will that feel? How will it feel to discuss blueprints and kitchens after I know what she feels like in my arms? What she tastes like? Because, son of a gun, though I made a couple of lame jokes about sex, how come it didn't occur to me that I can't spend the weekend standing stiffly beside her? Do that, and we won't convince cousin Violet of anything. I'm surely going to have to touch Bailey. Her hand. Her waist. I'll have to kiss her. Okay, maybe not on the mouth but on the temple. The cheek. And—who am I kidding? Of course, on the mouth! Boyfriend. Girlfriend. One generally shows affection for the other.

I remember the feel of Bailey's hair curling around my finger. The feel of her lips under mine. The whisper of her breath, the slightness of her body hidden inside those overalls, the sudden realization that she has all the right female parts...

Crap.

She has the right female parts. And I have the right male parts. One inside my pants, for sure. The one that's just come to immediate attention.

I have a hard-on. A massive one. And that's saying something because among my other attributes, I am what you would call well-hung. No, I'm not boasting. I'm the guy who buys those extra-large size condoms not to impress the drugstore clerk who rings them up but because I need them. And sometimes, at urinals...I know you've probably got this vision of an endless line of dudes taking peeks while they take leaks, but we do not look. Never. Except sometimes a guy's eyes stray, only by accident, and when they stray to me, well, I know what that little start of surprise means.

So this hard-on cannot be ignored.

Nor can the fact that thinking about my PA caused it.

Hell.

She's my PA. My assistant. I'm going away with her for the weekend to get even with Cousin Violet Who Once Killed A Doll Named Suzy, not because I have the hots for Bailey. I mean, Bailey's good people. She's sweet, she's smart, and she's efficient. What she isn't, is hot.

I close my eyes. I think of her in one of her suits, her hair yanked back, and I carefully rearrange myself.

There you go. No more hard-on. No more worries. Time to head home and get ready for our date. Our appointment. Because that's all it is.

TRAFFIC IS FAIRLY light and I'm in the city in no time. One of the reasons I bought the place in the West Village is that it has a garage big enough for my Harley as well as the 'Vette. No 'Vette this time. The truck tightens things up a little, but I manage.

The other reason I bought the place is that it has a garden. It's pretty private—high brick walls, a couple of tall sycamores. I like spending time there and so does Walter, my mastiff, who greets me the way he always does, all little woofs of happiness and head-butts and, for a grand finale, he puts those huge paws on my chest and gives me a sloppy kiss.

I let him into the garden. Normally I'd walk him, but I'm in kind of a hurry so I let him do his thing beside one of the sycamores while I wait, plastic baggie in hand.

We go back inside and I give him fresh water and his dinner—dry kibbles that have pictures of chickens and fish on the bag. Only the best for my boy. Last winter, I asked Bailey to do some research and find out which was the most nutritious brand of dog chow and...

And, damn, what else does she know about me?

I have a lot of catching up to do if we're gonna make this work.

"Woof!"

It's Walter, standing next to me with his front paws on the counter. Taking him to obedience school was a success because at the beginning of our relationship, he thought the way to do this was to stretch out one of his paws and drag his bowl off the counter's edge.

Now he simply observes.

"Woof," he says again, reminding me that I didn't do takeout last night. I went out to dinner, to one of my favorite places a few blocks away where the staff knows me, knows Walter, and always boxes up my leftovers and a few scraps of sirloin or chicken or whatever's on the menu for me to...

"Shit!"

Walter cocks his head and gives me an inquiring look.

"Not you, boy," I say as I get last night's leftovers from the fridge and take a look. "Looks like prime rib," I say.

Walter wags his entire body as I mix up the kibble and the beef and put the bowl down in front of him.

Last night's dinner.

With last night's date.

We'd gone out for the first time—I met her at a party a couple of weeks ago—and last night was fine. In fact, I'm supposed to be seeing her this Friday evening. And, if things went well, Saturday morning...

But I'll be in Schenectady. Or Troy. Or wherever it is that Cousin Violet and Elevator Boy with the box of laundry detergent lurk.

I take out my phone. Check my contacts. Make the call.

"Hey," I say brightly, "it's Matt. Yeah. Yes. I'm glad. I had a great time too. Uh, listen. About Friday..."

She's not happy. I can tell. But I don't lie. I tell her the Boy-Scout-Three-Fingers-Raised-in-Salute truth.

I tell her something's come up, a family thing, and I have to cancel our date.

I just don't tell her that the family thing has nothing to do with my family.

I Google Bailey.

I don't find her.

The good news is that it's not safe for a woman's address to be public.

The bad is that now I have no idea how to locate her. I know she lives in Manhattan. It's where singles seem to gather. I don't want to phone her and admit that I just flunked the first test about how much knowledge I have of her.

Wait.

I own O'Malley Design and Construction. I am its CEO. We have a website, sure, but we also have data stored in the Cloud. I log in, type in my password, hunt through files...

Bailey Abrams. And—it figures—she lives on the Upper West Side, which is where you live if you're into art, serious books, antique shops and museums. Culture with a Capital C.

I shower. Change into fresh jeans, a black tee, my old Roper boots. I check the mirror. How do I look...

Jesus H. Christ.

I'm not going to be spending the evening with a woman.

I'm spending it with my PA.

Walter knows I'm going out. I don't know how he knows, but he always does. He's sulking on the sofa in the den. Another benefit of obedience school. He learned to stretch out on the sofa instead of trying to stuff his one hundred fifty pounds into my favorite chair.

I rub his head, scratch him behind his ears, grab my old leather bomber jacket and my keys, and I'm gone.

Two seconds later, I'm back.

I said I'd bring dinner. On the Harley? Not the best

plan considering that I'm gonna have to get lots of different kinds of stuff since I don't know what Bailey likes.

Better take the truck.

And—man, I am not thinking straight—better phone for food first.

Forty-five minutes later, I arrive at Bailey's place. She lives in what was probably once a townhouse that's been cut up into apartments. Four steps up to the front door, then I'm in a small vestibule with a directory on the left hand wall.

B. Abrams. Apt. 4C.

I press the button under her name.

"Yes?" Bailey's electronic voice says.

"It's me."

"Who?"

I roll my eyes, but she's just being cautious. "Matthew."

She buzzes me in. I enter a tiny lobby, if you can call it that. Wonderful. There's no elevator. I have two enormous shopping bags; she lives on the fourth floor.

And I am—

"Late," she says when she opens the door.

"I know. Sorry. There's no place to park on this..." I look at her and I guess I frown. "What are you wearing?"

She looks at me like I'm nuts. "What do you mean, what am I wearing?"

It was a redundant question. I can see what she's wearing. One of those suits of hers. Not black. That was the suit du jour. This one is navy. She's tamed her hair into submission.

She looks as if she's ready for an evening with a roomful of tax accountants.

"Is that what you'd wear for a date?"

"This isn't a date. You said so yourself. It's a study session."

"It is. Yes. But it's also a date dry run. Please change into something you'd wear to spend a quiet evening at home with a boyfriend."

She opens her mouth, starts to speak...and turns on her heel, marches through the narrow hall, through what appears to be a living room, down another hall.

A door slams.

She's gong to change into something suitable for a quiet evening with a boyfriend.

I let my thoughts run wild over the possibilities: Silk pj's. A silk caftan. A slinky silk T and silk pants. Yes, I like silk. The way it feels, the way it clings...

Then I remember that this is Bailey and I roll my eyes, find the kitchen, and unload a dozen containers of food on the counter.

There's a noise behind me.

I turn around.

It's Bailey. And, goddammit, my jeans are suddenly tight.

No silk. Certainly not. She's wearing what I think women call yoga pants. Grey ones. And a T-shirt. It's grey too and it says—it's really washed out so it's hard to read, but I think it says *Unions. The People Who Brought You Weekends.* It's also small—must be all those washings—

so it's a little snug across what I am now absolutely, positively certain are breasts, and when she inhales, the bottom of the T rises a little, just enough so I can see that has, oh man, she has a little inny of a belly button.

Her feet are bare. She has pale pink polish on her toes.

And her hair is loose.

It's a long cloud of soft, dark curls.

She doesn't look sexy; she looks adorable. She looks like a woman you want to scoop into your arms. What I'm trying to say is that, yeah, she looks sexy, sexy as hell in her own way, and...

Fuck.

It's hard-on time again.

I swing away from her. Fast. "We need plates," I say briskly. "And silverware."

Drawers open and shut. Cabinet doors do the same. I hear things being put on a little table behind me. Uh oh. Maybe *put* is the wrong word. *Slammed* is more accurate.

I take a deep breath, think about icy fjords and snow, and then I turn around.

"Something wrong?" I say, very carefully.

"Why would anything be wrong?"

The better question is, why would a woman try to form words through her teeth?

"Bailey. I should have said you look fine."

Her back is to me. Her spine is a rigid line. So are her shoulders.

"I told you this wouldn't work!"

"Of course it will—"

I wince as a handful of forks and knives hit the table with the force of a tornado.

"Put on what you'd wear for an evening at home, you said."

"Right. A quiet evening with a boyfriend."

She spins towards me. Her eyes are flashing. I never knew my PA's eyes could flash and now that I do, I see that I was right the first time. Her irises are brown, not black, but it's such a dark brown, an espresso brown...

"What did you expect, Mr. O'Malley? Something from a Victoria's Secret catalogue?"

"No. Of course not."

"Of course not," she mimics, folding her arms over those I-didn't-realize-they-were-breasts breasts.

"No." I run my hand through my hair. "I mean, wait. You're taking this wrong."

"Oh, I saw that look."

"What look?"

"I saw how you reacted to the sight of me."

Jesus, I hope not!

"Bailey. You're dead wrong. You look great."

She makes a sound somewhere between 'pshaw' and what Walter says right before he heaves.

"You do," I tell her. "You look wonderful. Any man would be..."

"What man? I don't have one, remember? That's what started this entire stupid thing!"

"Well, you don't have one now. But any guy you

ever, you know, you were ever with, dated, any boyfriend in the past..."

"Did you really tell me you went to NYU, Mr. O'Malley? Because that had to be a lie. I don't think somebody as stupid as you could graduate from—from Degree-Mill U, let alone NYU."

"Degree-Mill U?" I laugh. Wrong move, but I can't help it. "Listen, Bailey—"

"No." She stalks towards me, chin raised, eyes glittering. Damn, she looks magnificent! "No, *you* listen!" One hand rises, forms into a fist with just the index finger sticking out. She jabs that index finger into the center of my chest. "I-have-no-boyfriend. I have *never* had a boyfriend. And if I did, I would have no idea what to wear for one of what you and the editors at Cosmopolitan call quiet nights at home. Get it?"

"Got it," I say, and the next thing I know, I'm reaching for her and pulling her into my arms.

She's warm. Soft. Her hair smells like a summer day. Flowers. Sunshine. Lemons.

Her hand, the one doing the jabbing, flattens against my chest.

And I bend my head and my mouth is on hers and the kiss is amazing, *amazing*, sweet and tender and innocent, except her lips are parting and I play the tip of my tongue over the fullness of her bottom lip and that hard-on is with me again...

I let go of her. She stumbles back. Our eyes meet. I need to apologize, to promise her this won't happen again, that it was a mistake.

She licks her lips, as if to take in the taste of me.

My dick salutes, and I turn away. Fast.

Impossible. This is going to be impossible. My brilliant plan to help her deal with Cousin Violet and Elevator Boy is not going to work...

"I know you had to do that. Eventually, I mean."

I blink and turned towards her. She's looking at me in a way that takes me back to seventh grade, a birthday party at Laura Devlin's house, all of us downstairs in the Devlin's finished basement playing Truth or Dare. I don't remember what my truth was, only that I ended up taking the dare, which was Laura and me stepping into the unfinished part of the basement and kissing.

The same expression that was on Laura's face is on Bailey's, a mixture of confusion, worry, anxiety...

And something I'd been too young to identify.

But I'm old enough to identify it now.

It's—it's pleasure.

"Right?" she says.

I blink again. "Right?"

"Yes. I'm right about what, you know, what just happened. You, kissing me." She blushes. "So we can do our best to pull this off."

"To pull this off?"

"To fool everybody next weekend."

"To fool..." I catch myself just in time. Did that pathetic excuse for a kiss turn me into a parrot? I inhale. Exhale. Smile. At least, I hope what's on my face is a smile. "Oh. Yes. Exactly. There'll have to be some contact between us. Holding hands. Me putting my arm around you."

"Kissing," she says, and she does that little tip-of-her-tongue thing again, and what the fuck is with my dick? It's doing its best to force its way through my zipper.

"Kissing," I say, pretty much the way the guy who does the nightly weather would say showers.

She nods. "Okay. But next time...Next time, I'd appreciate it if you could warn me. Just so I'm prepared."

"No problem."

We stare at each other. Then I hear myself tell her that since I didn't know what she wanted for dinner, I picked up a bunch of different things.

Silence. A long silence. Then she says what a good idea, or something like that, and together we finish emptying the bags and opening the containers until the counter looks like an international buffet. Lasagna. Pizza. A big green salad. Kung Pao chicken. Pad Thai. And, as an afterthought, a huge order of cheese-drenched nachos.

We both reach for the nachos. We smile and start munching.

"Good," she says.

I nod in agreement. "Always."

And neither of us mentions what happened just a few minutes ago.

HER CAT PUTS in a cautious appearance. It's a Siamese with slightly crossed eyes. Having it stare at me is kind of disconcerting because that off-kilter gaze is unblinking.

"Her name is Priscilla," Bailey says.

"Nice name." I squat down. "Come say hello, Priscilla."

The cat doesn't move. Or rather she does, but it's only to sit on her haunches and wrap her long chocolate tail around her feet.

"She's shy."

"Yeah." I stand up. "I can see that."

We talk cats for a few minutes. Then we tuck into pretty much everything on the counter.

Turns out she loves Thai and Chinese and Italian. Tex-Mex, she isn't sure about, but this is Tex-Mex from a place I know in the East Village and she says it might just turn her into a convert.

"So," I say, "I've learned something about you already. You're not a picky eater."

"No. Not at all."

That's gonna turn out to be an overstatement, but I won't find it out until our next meal together. For now, we're doing fine.

We clean up after dinner, arguing over who gets to keep the leftovers. I offer the winning argument: that my dog will pig out on anything I bring home and he's got to watch his boyish figure.

She laughs. She has a nice laugh. Open, easy, not in the least bit phony or self-conscious. I never thought about it before, but most women seem to be cautious about how they laugh. Not Bailey.

"Okay," she says. "I'll keep it all. There's enough here for dinner straight through the rest of the week."

"No," I say quickly. Her eyebrows rise. "I mean, we'll be having dinner together the entire week. What's left of it, anyway. Have to get to know each other, remember?"

"Every night?"

"Every night," I say firmly.

She frowns. Nibbles on her bottom lip. My eyes lock on the motion. When she stops nibbling, I drag my gaze to hers.

"I can't let you bring supper in every night, Mister...Matthew."

We've passed some sort of hurdle, though the use of my name is accompanied by a quick blush. Man. What is it with me? She touches the tip of her tongue to her lip, she chews on it, she blushes and, wham, my one-eyed monster gets to his feet and says *hello*.

"Fine. We'll go out for dinner."

"Go out?"

"Sure. We have to do that anyway. You know, get accustomed to being together in public."

"Oh."

"We can decide on the time tomorrow. In the office."

"No," she says emphatically. "In the office, we'll continue being what we always were. Always are. Still are, still will be after next weekend..." She stops. "Nobody should know about—about this."

She's right. I have a couple of fairly large construction crews, but my office staff is relatively small. Bailey.

Jack, our accountant. Beverly, the receptionist. Tony, who handles the endless paperwork you have to file to put up a house. We're a tight group and there's no way I'd want them gossiping about the boss, even if all I'm doing is giving Bailey a helping hand in her private life.

"I agree. Work as usual, at the office. So I'll pick you up tomorrow night at seven. Is that good?"

She nods, but I can see her hesitating.

"What?" I ask.

"What shall I wear?"

Women ask this question all the time. It usually means, are we going someplace expensive? Are we going to a club? Do I dress up? Dress down? Wear designer jeans or some short, tight thing that's laughingly called a dress? I understand this. Not only have I been dating for years, I grew up with a sister. I can remember the overheard telephone conversations girls have.

Should I wear the blue skirt with the white top? Jeans with heels or with boots? Should I put my hair up or down? That sweater I bought, remember? Should I wear it over a cami?

I remember wondering what in hell a cami was, but I knew better than to ask.

Those conversations would go on and on, pretty much ad nauseum. Dudes think about what to wear maybe half an hour before getting into the shower. Worrying over what to wear is a female thing.

Except, looking at Bailey, I kind of know none of the usual stuff is going through her head. What she means is exactly what she's asking. What should she wear? She's clueless. And I'd bet there's not much in her closet that she'd figure was appropriate for dinner out, aside from those awful suits.

As far as that goes, I'd be happy if she wore exactly what she's wearing right now. The yoga pants that show off long legs and hint at what I suspect is a sweetly rounded ass. The little T-shirt that's maybe half a size too small and just a little too short, and did I mention that when I kissed her and she got up on her toes, the shirt rode up just enough so I could feel the smooth skin of her belly against me?

The one-eyed beast gives my zipper another little nudge.

"Wear whatever you want," I say. I sound a little hoarse, so I smile to counteract it, drop a brotherly kiss on the top of her head and get the hell out while I still can.

6

W e are fine at the office the next day. In fact, we are too fine.

We're back to me being Mr. O'Malley or sir, and though I waggle my eyebrows a couple of times by way of suggesting she's not supposed to call me that anymore, my efficient PA ignores me.

Mid-morning, when she brings me a mug of coffee as she always does, I say a loud "Thank you" followed by a hissed "No more Mr. O'Malley, remember?"

Bailey frowns. She reaches for the notepad on the corner of my desk and writes something. Then she turns the pad towards me.

That change does not apply to business.

"That's ridiculous!"

Her frown deepens. She grabs the pad and scribbles again.

I have never addressed you so informally. It's improper.

I start to respond. Her frown becomes a glare. I roll my eyes and write furiously on the pad.

Improper? This is the year 2017. And have you ever noticed that EVERYONE else in this place calls me Matt???

It's Bailey's turn. She spins the pad towards her, writes something, then spins the pad back towards me.

You told me to call you Matthew.

She's right. I did.

Why would I call you Matthew, she writes, *when everyone else calls you Matt?*

It's a good question. I could tell her I was wrong, that she should call me Matt. But I don't want her calling me Matt. I don't want her calling me what everyone else calls me, and I'll be damned if I know the reason.

I open my mouth, then shut it. Bailey flashes me an I-told-you-so smile.

"Will there be anything else, *sir*?" she says.

I have a quick image of me saying yes, yes there will be something else, and then getting up from my desk, slamming shut the office door, grabbing my PA, stripping her out of today's suit choice—a particularly sexless dark grey with narrow white pinstripes—bending her over my desk and fucking her until she's incapable of saying anything except *Matthew, Matthew, Matthew* over and over and over...

"Not a thing," I say, very calmly, and I look at my computer monitor and start hitting the letters on my keyboard, and I don't dare look up again until I know Bailey's left my office.

Then I stop punching keys, grab my coffee and take a long swallow.

Maybe this plan of mine to help her take on Vicious Violet wasn't so smart.

For reasons beyond me to comprehend, it's not going quite the way it should.

WE GET THROUGH THE MORNING.

I have a lunch appointment with the couple determined to build the wrong house on the right property. When I leave, Bailey is at her desk eating something that looks like granola and yogurt from a plastic cup.

"I'll be back by two," I say.

"Very good, Mr. O'Malley."

I start down the hall. Then I stop and walk back to her desk.

"What is that stuff?" I ask.

"Granola," she says. "And yogurt."

I nod and make a mental note to my growing list of Things I Know Abut Bailey. Despite last night's foray into a United Nations assortment of food, she is a health nut. Or maybe not. Maybe she prefers what any civilized American would call real food, but she figures it's improper to indulge in it.

Propriety seems to be a big thing for my PA.

Which makes me wonder how she'd react if she knew there's a tiny drop of yogurt on her upper lip. I'm sure she'd deem it improper.

Meaning, I have three choices.

I can ignore it.

I can tell her about it and hand her a tissue—she has a box of them on her desk.

Or I can lean down and lick that drop away.

A shot of heat goes from my balls to the top of my head.

"What?" she says, and for half a second I wonder if she sees flames shooting out of my fly.

"Nothing," I say crisply. "I just—I just—I forget something."

She pushes back her chair. "Tell me what it is and I'll get it."

I wave my hand in the air. "Not necessary. It isn't important."

She looks puzzled. "But you said—"

"I'll see you at two," I say, and I turn my back to her and make my escape.

I MEET my would-be clients at a place tucked into the heart of Old Greenwich. The Scotts chose it and it's handsome and quiet, but it figures that it's all dark wood, spindle-top chairs, and enough potted plants so I expect to be handed a watering can instead of a wine glass. Still, the food is good, the wine is, too, and the Scotts are nice people. We have some general conversation over glasses of a Napa Valley cabernet sauvignon.

Then we get down to business.

Mostly it consists of me giving them all the reasons building the house they envision on those four acres would be a mistake. I talk about the rise of the land, the view out over a forest, the small lake and the untouched valley just beyond it. I tell them it all calls for something sleek with lots of glass, high ceilings and pale floors. When they don't say anything, I tell them I wish I could build their house for them, but I can't.

I can see I've finally gotten through.

Jim Scott puts his elbows on the table and steeples his fingers.

"We appreciate your honesty, Matt."

I shrug. "I'd be wrong to pretend that I share your vision for this house, Jim. And I know it sounds corny, but I think sharing a vision for a place is important."

The Scotts nod at each other. Jim looks at me. "Would it be possible for you to—"

"Recommend someone? Absolutely." I take a sheet of paper from my pocket. I've written two names and phone numbers on it. "Either of these guys would be excellent choices. Be sure and tell them I sent you."

Jim hands the paper to his wife. She tucks it into her pocketbook. Then we talk about stuff for another couple of minutes and Jim reaches for the check.

I get to it first.

"It's my pleasure," I say, and it truly is. I like this couple. I just don't like what they want to do with that land.

We stroll outside. My 'Vette is parked at the curb. Their car is in the lot behind the restaurant. We exchange handshakes, promises to keep in touch, and as I start towards my car I can hear the Scotts speaking softly to each other. I reach my car, unlock the door and start to climb in when Jim calls out to me. I turn around. He and his wife wave me over.

"Julie and I thought you'd like to know that we're going to call the realtor," he says, "and tell him we're giving up our option on the land."

I'm puzzled. "But you just asked me to recommend a builder."

"You convinced us," Julie Scott says, and smiles. "That land is for a different kind of house."

I'm pleased and I tell them so. We shake hands again and this time, just before we part company, Julie puts her hand lightly on my arm.

"I can't help but wonder," she says, "if you've ever thought of buying that land and building a house for yourself?"

I grin. "Nice idea, but I have a place. In Manhattan."

"Ah. I forgot. You're a bachelor. Of course you have a place in Manhattan. Why would you want to live on the top of a hill in the middle of nowhere?"

We all laugh politely.

Why, indeed? I think as I pull away from the curb.

Me, with a house in the middle of nowhere.

I shake my head, reach to the dashboard and punch a button. My 'Vette is restored to her original self, but I've added some new tricks. Like Bose speakers and satellite radio.

I fiddle with the stations until I find one that plays oldies. Aerosmith fills not just the car but my head. Still, that image of a house on a hill surrounded by forest is tough to shake.

Maybe in ten years. Or fifteen.

Aerosmith gives way to AC/DC, and I step down on the gas and let the Corvette do its thing all the way back to the office.

AT FIVE MINUTES OF SEVEN, I step from a taxi outside Bailey's apartment building. I hand the driver a bill and tell him to wait for me. He nods, leans back and settles in.

I go up the steps, enter the small vestibule, press the button for Bailey's apartment—and wait.

It gives me time to think about the choices I've made for tonight.

I hope they're correct.

I spent a lot of time planning our evening. For some reason, my approach to this thing hasn't been as businesslike as it should have been, so this afternoon I put in a couple of hours remedying that. I don't want Bailey to feel intimidated, so I've made reservations at a restaurant in the fifties that's not elegant but is definitely upscale. And I'm dressed down, not up. Jeans. Boots. A white broadcloth shirt open at the neck under a grey tweed jacket. I know. Tweed isn't in, but I like it, maybe because my Dad has always been a tweed guy.

And how come she hasn't buzzed me in? Could she have gotten cold feet and decided to call the whole thing off?

Bzzzz.

Okay. Here we go. I trot up the endless steps, hang a right and get to her door. It's cracked open.

I rap on it with my knuckles. "Bailey?"

"Yes. Come in."

I do, but she's nowhere to be seen. I shut the door behind me and make a mental note to warn her about leaving her door open. The buzzer system isn't really much of a deterrent against intruders.

"Bailey?" I say again.

"I'll be right there."

I stroll around her tiny living room. Don't I pay her enough for a bigger place? A place with an elevator? I'm pretty sure I do. On the other hand, what do I really know about rent in Manhattan now? After NYU, I moved into a flat near Wall Street. I shared it with two other guys and after my first bonus, I moved into a place of my own. And after that, I bought the town-house. Maybe I moved up too fast to pay enough attention to...

Mrrrow.

I look down. The Siamese is weaving between my ankles. What's her name? Prudence. Patience.

Priscilla.

She says *Mrrrow* again and keeps making those figure eights. And leaving cream-colored fur on my jeans. Well, what the heck, I think as I squat down and stroke her. Walter sheds too. His fur is darker so you don't see it as easily, but—

"Is this okay?"

I look up. And think, OMG! It's Bailey. And I don't

know which is worse—what she's wearing, or the look of desperation in her eyes.

It takes me less than a second to come up with the answer.

That look reaches right inside and does something funny to my heart.

"Hey," I say, smiling as I get to my feet.

"It's not, is it? All right, I mean."

Well, no. It's not. The good news? She's not wearing one of those suits. The bad? If one of those suits could give birth to a dress, this would be it.

The dress is, I don't know, it's like stripes. Horizontal stripes. And it's made of something chunky. Wrong word. Heavy. Still wrong, but hell, what do I know about fabric? This stuff is...thick. It looks like it could stand up all by itself. Plus, it's just—it's just not right. The sleeves go to her wrists. The neckline's so high I'm surprised she isn't gasping for breath. And the skirt...Same as any guy I'm a big fan of those little dresses that just about cover a woman's thighs, but okay, maybe not on Bailey. It wouldn't be right. Not that I don't think she's probably got great thighs—yeah, sure, I've given them a couple of minutes thought since last night, when those yoga pants or whatever you call them hinted at what was beneath...

How did I get off on this track?

The point is, Bailey's not the kind of girl you'd pick up in a bar. Or find on Tinder. I wouldn't want to see her ass when she bends over. Well, I would, but only if we were alone and we'll be in public tonight...And I didn't mean that about wanting to see her ass if we were alone. Or maybe I did. Because, really, I've spent enough time looking at her the past, what, twenty-four hours to know that she's an attractive woman. Easy on the eyes. Pretty...

Shit.

She's beautiful, if she'd just stop hiding behind the baggy clothes, the pulled-back hair, the clunky shoes...

They're not quite as clunky tonight, but they'd still qualify as the kind of shoes a woman would wear if she were heading off on a ten-mile march. And, yes, her hair is pulled back, secured low on her neck with a band. And before you think I've forgotten the length of that dress, I haven't. It's not thigh-high which, I've already said, is okay. It's not above-the-knee, which would fine. It's not right-below-the-knee, which wouldn't be great, but I could live with that.

The hem of this thing hits at mid-calf. My mom wears her skirts shorter than that.

"Matthew."

I look up. Her mouth is trembling.

"I bought this last year. For an aunt and uncle's fortieth anniversary party. It's the only dress-up thing I have."

"Don't tell me," I say carefully. "You were home. And Cousin Violet went shopping with you."

She nods. Her mouth trembles a little more.

"I look hideous," she says, and before I can think about it too long, I reach for her and pull her into my arms.

She's a little stiff at first and then she gives a muffled sob and leans into me.

My arms tighten around her.

She feels warm and soft.

The simple truth is, she feels wonderful.

I murmur some nonsense words, sort of the way I did one day when my little niece fell down and skinned her knees. I run one hand up and down Bailey's spine. Mostly, I just hold her.

I close my eyes. Damn, she smells good. And her hair, even plastered back the way it is, feels soft when I stroke my hand over it.

Instinctively, I pull off the elastic that's confining it. It tumbles free, a mass of curls that frame her face and shoulders.

She mumbles something. Reluctantly, I draw back a little and look down at her.

"I couldn't hear what you said," I tell her softly.

She looks up at me. "I said that this is never going to work."

Hers eyes are damp. Glittering with tears. Carefully, I wipe them away with my thumbs.

"Of course it is."

She shakes her head and looks down again. "We'll never fool anyone. I was wrong to think we could."

"Hey." I put a hand under her chin and raise her face to mine. "An NYU grad and a Columbia grad. With degrees in business and finance, surely two smart people like us can—"

"Medieval Lit."

"Huh?"

She sighs. "That was my major. Four years of

Beowulf and Chaucer, and do you know what happens when you graduate?"

"Well—"

"Nothing happens. There are zero jobs for people who study Medieval Lit. They end up waiting on tables. Working at Walmart. And they take out loans so they can go back to school for a year to study..."

"Business," I say.

She sighs. "Yes."

"Maybe it's karma," I tell her. "That some of us think we know what we want to study until it turns out we were wrong. I mean, I studied business. Well, finance, to be exact. And when I graduated, there were lots of jobs, all right, but it turned out it wasn't anything that made me happy."

"And building houses does?"

"Yeah."

She manages a wobbly smile. "I thought I was the only person who wasted four years."

"You didn't waste anything."

"Of course I did."

"Did you enjoy Medieval Lit?"

"Yes, I loved it."

"Then studying it wasn't a waste."

"Cousin Violet said—"

I put my finger across her lips. Man, her lips are soft!

"Never mind what Cousin Violet said. Life is short. If you find something that gives you pleasure, go with it."

"So, how did that work for you? Did you at least get pleasure from studying Finance?"

"Yeah. I did. I have this thing for numbers, you know? They're fun. And without that degree, I'd never have made enough money to quit and go back to school to study what I really wanted." I run my finger lightly over her mouth. I've dated a couple of women with lips that you just know have been shot full of whatever that shit is that makes them plump. Touch those, it's kind of like when you were a kid visiting your grandma and you'd sit down on the sofa and feel as if the cushions were going to swallow you.

Anyway, you get my meaning. Artificial softness isn't so great.

Real softness is.

And my PA's lips are real. And really, really soft. And her eyes are still damp, the lashes anyway, the very long, dark lashes...

I bend my head and kiss her.

An easy kiss. A tender one.

Her eyes close. She draws in her breath.

It's as if it's me she's drawing in.

I step back. "Okay," I say briskly, and she blinks her eyes open. "Okay," I say again. "Let's see what we can do with this outfit."

Wrong thing to say, even for a guy who can, at this moment, barely think coherently. Her mouth trembles again. I think about stopping that trembling with another kiss.

Instead, I turn brisk and businesslike.

"Nothing wrong with it," I tell her. "We just need to, uh, to nudge it along."

"How?"

How, indeed? I step back and look her over. Her face colors a little under my scrutiny. I squat down and finger the hem. She starts to jerk back and I frown up at her and tell her to stand still.

The material is, as I said, chunky. Wrong word. It's —it's substantial. It has heft to it. I bet if you cut off part of the hem, nobody would notice that you'd done it.

Hell. Why not? And we don't have time to waste. A quick look at my watch tells me we're due at the restaurant in forty minutes.

I stand up. "Scissors."

"What for?"

"Bailey. Just get me a pair of scissors, okay?"

She looks at me as if I'm nuts. Then she turns and heads for the kitchen where she opens a drawer and takes out a big pair of scissors.

"Great," I say, as if I know what I'm doing. "Okay. Climb up on that chair."

"Mr. O'Malley—"

"Ms. Abrams. Get up on that chair."

She makes a face, but she steps up on the chair. I hold out my hand to help her and I get a flash of leg.

A very nice flash.

The legs go with the rest of her. Shapely. Firm. Not scrawny, even though I know that scrawny is in. I like my women with a little meat on their bones. Not that Bailey is my woman. Well, she is, but only as a loaner...

Jesus, O'Malley, stay with the program!

"Matthew! What are you doing?"

What I am doing is cutting away part of the dress. The skirt. I'm cutting along the bottom of a blue stripe. I step back and take a look. Not enough. The strip above it is pale blue. I cut it away. Still not enough.

"Matthew..."

"Stand still. I'm almost finished."

Not true. I slice away half a dozen stripes, which is maybe eight inches of skirt. Now the hem is just a couple of inches above her knees, and I have a great view of knees, calves and ankles. It's all prime real estate—and the lady in question is sputtering.

I put aside the scissors, grab her by the waist and lift her down. She yanks free, eyes the cut-off stuff on the floor and then looks at me as if I'm certifiable.

"What did you do?"

She asks it pretty much the way a horrified bystander would ask Godzilla what he did to Tokyo.

"Do you have a mirror? A full length mirror?"

"Yes. In the bedroom. But—"

I grab her hand and hurry her out of the kitchen, through the hall and to the door at the end. Her bedroom. It stops me for a minute. It's, well, it's not Bailey. Or maybe it's just not the Bailey I thought I knew all these years, because that Bailey would not have a room done in white and what I guess you'd call peach, with multiple pillows strewn over the bed and —what do you call that thing coming down the sides of the mattress, some kind of ruffled skirt. There are silver candlesticks on the dresser across from the bed with peachy-colored candles in them...

And while I'm standing there gaping, she frees her hand, walks to a closet, opens the door and yup, there's a mirror.

She looks at me.

I signal that she should turn around and look at herself, not at me. She hesitates, takes a deep breath, turns, and...

She claps her hands to her face. "My skirt is gone!"

I laugh. "It's not gone."

"You left most of it on the floor in the living room!"

"I left the part you don't need on the floor in the living room."

She shakes her head wildly from side to side. "It's too short."

"It's just right."

And it is. For the third time in the past five minutes, I notice she has great legs. In fact, I bet she has great everything else, if we can just get to see some of it.

"What's under the jacket?"

"The dress, of course."

"Not a, you know, a shirt?"

"A blouse? No. It's a dress. But—"

I walk up behind her, turn her around, and reach for the buttons on the jacket. Her hands slap at mine.

"What are you doing?"

"I want to see the dress."

"You're not supposed to see it. That's the reason for the jacket."

"Then why isn't it just a suit instead of a dress?"

She stares at me. "Because it isn't a suit. It's a—"

"Exactly. It's a dress. Jacket optional."

"You're supposed to wear them together."

"Fashion advice from Violet the Vile?"

I can see she doesn't want to laugh, but she does. Meanwhile, I begin undoing buttons.

One. Two.

I can see her throat. It's lovely throat, long and smooth-looking, with a rapid beat in the hollow.

Three. Four.

Better and better. The dress actually begins just above her breasts. In fact...

Five. Six.

In fact, I can hardly breathe. I've revealed the swell of her breasts. The lush curve. The start of the delicate shadow between them.

"Matthew," she says in a whisper.

"Shhh," I say, and slowly I ease the jacket back. I can see the narrow straps that hold the dress on her shoulders. I ease the jacket back further. It slides away and falls to the floor.

I was wrong when I said she was beautiful.

She isn't just beautiful. She's gorgeous. She's Goldilocks personified. Not too much. Not too little. She's just right

I say her name. She says nothing; she just stares at me wide-eyed. I say her name again. I want to reach for her. Take her in my arms. Hell. What I want is to reach behind her, unzip the dress...

"Matthew," she says, her voice barely a whisper, and I know I could do it, she would let me do it, she would let me strip her naked so I could kiss her, taste her, her breasts, her belly, her thighs...

So you could take advantage of her, you mean. Because that's what you'd be doing. She knows zilch about the world, about men. That's why you're here, pal, or maybe you forgot that this isn't real. You're doing this for her. Remember?

The voice is clear and cold inside my head. The message is valid. One hundred percent valid. I take a deep breath and step back; I pin what I hope is a big smile on my face.

"There," I say. "Perfect."

She runs the tip of her tongue over her bottom lip. Man, I wish she wouldn't do that.

"Really?"

I grab her hand and turn her toward the mirror. "Look."

She looks. In fact, she stares. I watch her face, trying to read what she's thinking. Is the skirt too short? Does the dress show too much? I wasn't this nervous waiting to see my first bonus check back in the days when I was a hedge fund hotshot who could do no wrong.

She lifts her hand. Touches her hair. "I never wear my hair loose," she says.

"Well, you should."

"And the skirt..."

"Not short enough?" I say innocently.

She looks at me in the mirror. "Very funny."

"It's fine."

She looks uncertain and I think about taking her in my arms. Just for comfort, of course...

Have you noticed that I'm a bad liar?

"Okay," I say briskly, "time to get moving. Our reservation's for eight o'clock...What?"

This time, she's not touching her tongue to her lip. She's sinking her teeth into it. Very gently. I could do it even more gently.

"My shoes."

I clear my throat. "Your shoes?"

She nods. I look down at her feet. She's right. Those serviceable clodhoppers definitely don't make it with her new look.

"Before you ask," she says, "I don't have anything with, you know, a different kind of heel."

Hell. I look at my watch again. What we need is a shoe store, but we're running out of time. I know the owner of the restaurant we're going to, but I want us to have a leisurely dinner. Plus, I have a bad feeling about getting her into a place where she'll be faced with a zillion choices in shoes. Still, what else can we do?

"Okay," I tell her. "We'll make a stop on the way. Saks is still open."

She blanches. Actually, I've never used that word before. It always struck me as, I don't know, overdone. But there's no other word to describe Bailey's reaction except to say that she blanches.

"Not Saks," she says.

"Why not Saks?"

"I—I don't know. I mean, I'm not dressed for Saks..."

"Did we or did we not agree you look great?"

"You're just saying that to make me feel better."

"Bailey. You've been with me for, what, six years? By now you surely know that I speak my mind. If I say you look great, it's because you do."

She hesitates. "Really?"

"Really," I say, and when I see the wariness in her eyes I do the only natural thing a man can do in this kind of situation. I lean in and kiss her. That's all I do. My mouth on her mouth. No tongue. No pressure. It doesn't last much more than a tenth of a second.

But stepping away from her is almost painful.

7

She ditches the jacket of the dress for a scarf. It's not bad, but it's not the kind I'd choose for her —but there's no time to worry about that now.

Shoes are what we have to worry about.

The cabbie gets us to Saks in what has to be world-class time. I grab Bailey's hand and we hurry inside. I have no idea where women's shoes are located. I've been here before, but only to buy shirts and ties for myself and sometimes Christmas or birthday gifts for my mom and sister. Pocketbooks. Perfume. Jewelry. And, okay, jewelry a couple of times for women I was dating. And, yes, some lace undies. Lingerie, women call that stuff.

But shoes?

No way.

A clerk tells me we want the eighth floor. The elevator takes us up—and as we step from the car, I hear Bailey make a little sound you can only call a moan.

I can't blame her.

We are facing a sea of elegance.

I start moving.

Bailey stands still.

I reach back, clasp her hand and all but drag her forward. A saleswoman glides towards us. She's middle-aged, perfectly put-together, all smiles, and when she reaches us and says "Good evening," I'm not the least surprised that the words are delivered in plummy British tones.

"Good evening," I answer.

"How may I help you?"

Her gaze sweeps over Bailey and pauses at the shoes on Bailey's feet. I can almost hear the lady's eyebrows shoot into her hairline. Her next stop is at the hem of Bailey's dress.

Uh oh.

I see half a dozen dangling threads at the hem I created half an hour ago. So does our saleswoman. The job now is to keep Bailey from seeing them as well.

"We need a pair of shoes," I say.

"Flats?" says the Pretender to the British Throne.

"Heels."

"Matthew," Bailey says quietly.

I squeeze her hand. "Really high. Black. Or whatever you think will go best with my, ah, my fiancée's dress."

"I'm not—"

I squeeze Bailey's hand again. "As quickly as possible, please. "

The woman motions us to a pair of chairs. Bailey

sits and our salesclerk removes the right shoe from Bailey's foot. She reaches for one of those measuring things. Bailey waves it away.

"I'm an eight," she mumbles, as if the number is shameful. The work of Violet the Victimizer, I think, and I smile encouragingly at the clerk as I ease into the chair next to Bailey's.

"Eight," I say. "With what do you call them? Spiked heels."

Bailey starts to speak. I clasp her hand and bring it to my mouth. Just as I'd hoped, she falls silent. At least, she's silent until the Queen Mum walks away.

"Matthew," she hisses. "I won't be able to walk in heels like that. And telling that woman that I'm your fiancée..."

"You'll walk just fine. And tonight is all about getting comfortable with each other, remember? We might as well start here."

Bailey catches her bottom lip between her teeth. She does that a lot. How come I never noticed it before?

"Comfortable is one thing. But engaged..."

"Okay. We'll stick with that we're just dating."

"I wouldn't bring a man I was just dating to a wedding."

"People do. All the time. What's it called? A plus one."

"This is a family function, Matthew. I wouldn't bring a plus one to a family function."

She's right. She wouldn't. Women do, but Bailey

isn't *women*, she's Bailey, and she wouldn't take a casual date to a family wedding.

But that's just the point, I think, and that's what I say.

"But that's just the point, remember? We want Violet to think we're involved."

"I've been thinking about that."

"About what?"

"About pretending we're, you know, we're involved. It's one thing to fool Violet—but we'll be fooling my mom, too. I'm not sure that's the right thing to do."

She's going to back out. And, dammit, I don't want that to happen. I'm committed to this little charade. I'm enjoying it. I'm enjoying her. And, really, who can it harm?

I say that to Bailey. Not the part about enjoying it. Hell. Or about enjoying her. I tell her that if she seems happy next weekend, her mom will be happy. It's logical, but she looks unconvinced.

"It's not as if we're going to claim we're engaged or anything," I say, and before she can answer, our saleswoman is back. She has three boxes. She sits down before Bailey, who has already kicked off her shoes.

"Let's see what we have," the Queen says, and she says it gently, as if she knows this is going to be important and maybe even traumatic.

She opens all the boxes.

Bailey gasps. I shoot a glance at her. The expression on her face is the kind a guy hopes to see when his lady gets her first glimpse of his equipment. Women certainly have weird reactions to shoes. I mean, I've always heard they do, but this is reality TV at its best.

There's a pair of black suede things. Pumps, I think you call them. A pair of dark blue, what, sandals? Yeah. Sandals. Open back, open toes, straps around the ankle. And another blue pair, but this blue is the same color as one of the stripes on Bailey's dress. They're nothing but heels and narrow straps, and they look as if they're made of butterfly wings.

The heels on all of them are the kind that make men have wicked dreams and all of a sudden I begin to understand Bailey's gasp.

I also understand why she's shaking her head and I'm nodding mine.

"Just try one pair," I say.

The saleswoman holds out one of those butterfly wings. Bailey slips her foot in. The shoe goes on easily. So does its mate. There are a couple of straps to close and then The Pretender to the Throne sits back.

"See how they feel when you walk," she says.

When Bailey walks? I can hardly breathe, just looking at her sitting next to me. She's an amazing sight. Those endless legs. Those delicate shoes. Those icepick heels...

But she's not moving.

I rise to my feet. Hold out my hand.

She shakes her head. "I don't think I can."

"Of course you can." My voice is a little hoarse and I clear my throat. "Come on. Walk with me."

Gingerly, she takes my hand and stands.

I move forward. So does she. She wobbles a little. I

slide my arm around her waist. We take another couple of steps. She's a little more steady now. And she's moving differently. There's some hip action I never noticed before. She looks up at me. I tell her she's doing fine. We head for a mirror and when she sees herself, she gives a breathless little laugh.

"Wow," she says.

That just about sums it up.

My girl is spectacular.

My PA, I mean.

We pivot. Walk back to the saleswoman, who cocks her head and looks at me.

"What do you think, sir?"

I can't tell her what I think. It's X-rated because what I think is that those long, endless legs of Bailey's belong wrapped around my waist. Instead, I take out my wallet and hand over a credit card.

"Which pair?" she asks.

"We'll take all three," I say, and, despite Bailey's protests, we do. Bailey keeps on the butterfly wings and the store will deliver the other shoes, plus the ones she was wearing, to her apartment tomorrow.

Our salesclerk smiles, and I suspect it has little to do with the four-figure sale she's just made. It's a smile that turns her from the Queen Mum into Mary Poppins, and I smile back.

"Thank you," I say, and then we hurry to the elevator, Bailey swaying a little, and that sway is sexy as hell. When we reach the ground floor, I reach for her hand and I get jabbed in the side with her pocketbook. It's big enough to hold a week's worth of groceries. How come I didn't notice that before?

I tug her towards a display of tiny, glittery purses. A saleswoman beams at us.

"Matthew," Bailey says in a warning whisper, but I ignore her.

"May I help you?" the saleswoman purrs.

I look over the display. Time's racing by. We're already late, very late for our reservation.

"We'll take that one," I say, pointing at a small silver thing with a long strap.

"Matthew," Bailey says, "I don't need—"

"And that scarf. The blue and silver one."

"Matthew!"

I turn to her, smile and say, "Now, sweetheart, you know how much I love to give you pretty things.'

Bailey damn near bares her teeth. The saleswoman beams and hands the purse and scarf to me. I pull off Bailey's old scarf and drape the new one around her shoulders. Then I grab her pocketbook and empty it onto the counter. Stuff pours out. A comb. A lipstick. A wallet. Two things that are either hairclips or medieval torture devices. A small hairbrush. A phone. A tin of breath mints. A box of cough drops. A notepad. Two pens. A nail file. A folded up section of The New York Times. A ring of keys surely sufficient to open every door in Manhattan.

I dangle the keys in front of Bailey.

"Which one's for your apartment?"

"The silver one. But—"

I snap the silver key off the ring and drop it into the

little silver purse along with the phone, the comb, the wallet and one—just one— tissue. Everything else, including the old scarf, goes back into the old hand-bag. I hand over my credit card, give the saleswoman instructions to pack up the old pocketbook and have it delivered to Bailey's apartment tomorrow.

Then we're in the taxi again.

"You just spent three thousand four hundred and ninety eight dollars," Bailey hisses as we head into traffic.

"Three thousand four hundred and ninety eight dollars and forty-three cents," I say. "Or have you forgotten I'm hell with numbers?"

"I'll pay back every cent."

"Forget it."

"Forget it? FORGET IT? Do you honestly think I'd let you spend that much money and not repay it?"

"Consider it a bonus."

"O'Malley Design and Construction doesn't give bonuses."

"It does now."

"Mr. O'Malley—"

"We're not going to debate this. I'm the boss. I'm in charge. I get to decide if we offer bonuses or not. Understand?"

She shakes her head. "What I understand is that you're crazy!"

Maybe I am—but I'm having fun.

And maybe I'm lying to myself, but despite Bailey's words, there's a glint in her eyes that says maybe she is, too.

8

We arrive at the restaurant and we are, of course, late. Very late.

But as I said before, James, the owner and chef, is a guy I've known for a long time. When I give the maître d' my name, James comes out to greet us. He tells the maître d' to seat us at a table near the big gas fireplace that dominates the room. It's a coveted spot, not just because of the fireplace but because of its privacy, and I thank him.

"My pleasure," he says.

We exchange some polite words and then he waves away the maître d' and tells us about the evening's special dishes. I listen with half an ear. Mostly, I watch Bailey. Her cheeks are flushed, her eyes are bright. There's a lovely little curve to her lips.

She's enjoying this place.

I hoped she would. That's why I chose it. It's the kind of restaurant she can name-drop to Cousin Violet —*The Manhattan Corner* is very well known—but mostly I figured she would like the atmosphere, that she'd feel comfortable here. And from the look on her face, I made a good choice.

James clears his throat and I realize he'd stopped speaking a couple of minutes ago.

"Thank you, James," I say. "Just give us a couple of minutes, okay?"

He smiles, assures us that there's no hurry and that he'll send over our waiter and the sommelier. The waiter arrives with menus, the wine guy with the wine list.

I look at Bailey. "Any idea what you'd like for dinner?" I ask, before I choose a wine.

She blinks. "I don't...Why don't you order for me, Matthew?"

I don't think a woman's ever asked me to do that before. It gives me a good feeling. Not that I think we should go back to the days when men ordered for their women, but there's something special about having that kind of trust put in your hands.

And, hell, I'm making ten times more out of this than it deserves.

It's probably just because this is a good first step. I mean, we agreed that we have to get comfortable with each other in public. Couples who are, well, couples behave differently than men and women who are just friends or who work together, or even couples that are dating.

In fact, we need to develop a vibe, something that hints at depth and—please let me not hyperventilate—possible permanency.

I've never been in that type of relationship, but I know that's the only thing that will mean anything to Violet the Vile and, more to the point, it's what will make Bailey's mother a believer. Bailey and I will know we're breaking up after the wedding, but nobody else will.

Well, we won't be breaking up.

I mean, there won't actually be anything to break up...

Fuck.

We just need to pull this off, and that means behaving a certain way. That I haven't participated in what people call a relationship doesn't mean I'm not observant.

I've noticed how people act.

So I smile, close the menu and tell the waiter we'll have the veal and—

"Not veal," Bailey says quickly. "I don't eat veal. Do you know what veal really is? How they raise it? What they—"

"No veal," I say. "We'll have the salmon. And—"

"As long as it isn't farmed. Farming is such a nice-sounding word, but the truth is that—"

Bailey falls silent. She's looking at the waiter. The waiter and I both look at her. Color rises in her cheeks, but her voice is strong.

"...the truth is that they're raised in confinement. And they're fed chemicals. And—"

"What would you prefer?" I ask.

She does it again. The teeth. The bottom lip. Is she determined to drive me crazy?

"Anything," she says blithely. "Your choice."

Oh-kay.

I think of the stuff we ate last night. Lasagna. Pizza. Pad Thai. Nachos. So she's not a vegan or a vegetarian, she's just, what, environmentally aware, if that's the current term, and I think it is.

I look at the menu again. I think back to the specials James mentioned. Something about a porterhouse for two. That seems safe enough... No. I'm pretty sure the place serves Kobe beef and a little voice in my head whispers that ranchers or whatever you call them who raise Kobe cattle give the animals massages to make sure the meat will be tender when they're, uh, when they're, uh, harvested...

Jesus Christ. No more Kobe beef for me. And, man, I am lost here.

"We have a lovely eggplant Parmesan," the waiter says into the yawning silence.

Eggplant. Purple on the outside. Green on the inside. No food should be purple, and only lettuce should be green.

But Bailey is looking at me. I try not to shudder.

"Amazing," I say briskly. "That's exactly what I was going to suggest."

THE EGGPLANT TURNS out to be okay.

It'll never replace prime rib, but it's edible. Maybe it's even good. I can't tell, because I'm too caught up in conversation with my PA. Politics. A comedy skit on

SNL it turns out neither of us understood. Nothing big, but it's fun to talk with her and I don't really pay much attention to the food, even when we get to dessert.

Which is, mercifully, not a problem.

Maybe our waiter clued his boss in, because James brings our dessert himself, no questions asked: two glorious dishes of something he calls Strawberry Chouf, which turns out to be a melt-in-your-mouth pastry filled with gelato and strawberries, all topped with whipped cream.

"Umm," Bailey sighs at the first bite, and when she licks a tiny crumb off her top lip, I have to look away.

"So," I say briskly, "you like classical music."

She nods. "Especially orchestral stuff. You know. Symphonies." She hesitates. "But I like other kinds too."

"For instance?"

"Eric Clapton. He's amazing."

We agree. He is. What's equally amazing is that after a little more prodding, she admits she likes Neil Young. And Bonnie Raitt.

I get the crazy feeling this is the kind of thing she doesn't tell many people. One secret deserves another, so I admit that after my folks took me to a July Fourth concert in some park out on Long Island when I was maybe twelve or thirteen, I went online and downloaded *The 1812 Overture.*

"Tchaikovsky," she says with delight.

"Yeah. You know it?"

She laughs. "I can play it!"

I laugh along with her. "What? The cannon part?"

She makes a face. "Very funny. No, not the cannon part. But the rest...I played the flute when I was in school."

I can see it. Hear it. She's the perfect girl for an instrument that makes such soft, sweet sounds. Hey, I'm not a complete barbarian. I know what a flute sounds like.

"Do you still play?" I ask.

"I haven't. Not in years." She does the teeth-into-the-lip thing. "But I still have that flute, packed away somewhere."

It's time for an obvious joke. A reference to the flute. The skin flute. Except, I don't want to make jokes like that. Not with her. Not involving her. Instead, I pour us some more wine—I ordered Montrechat, did I mention that? I pour, and I tell her that in my salad days, I was hell on guitar.

She smiles. Lifts her glass. Sips at her wine. "I bet you had a band."

I grin. "We called it Passport." She looks puzzled. "We wanted to be Journey or Foreigner, but both names were already taken, so we settled on—"

"Passport. Of course." She laughs. Then she sighs. "That all seems long ago, doesn't it? High school. Worrying about getting A's. Football." She makes a face. "Proms."

"I bet you never had to worry about getting A's."

She shakes her head. "No. Not really."

"And I bet you were never much for going to football games."

"I never understood the fuss."

I nod. "And proms. Never my thing. I mean, renting a tux? Buying a corsage? Drinking spiked punch and puking your guts up in the rented limo on the way to Lookout Point?"

"Did you? Puke in the limo?"

I laugh. "No. I made it out before it happened."

We both laugh. Then her laughter fades. Did she not go to her prom? I don't want to ask. Instead, I tell her that football is one of the greatest things we have in America.

It works. She gives one of those eye rolls, the kind she gave the last time we discussed the game.

"No way."

I get what seems like a brilliant idea. "You know what?"

"What?"

"We should have something we can share. Something we can talk about in public so people will believe we spend a lot of time together."

"For instance?"

"Football."

Bailey looks at me like I'm crazy. "Matthew. I just told you—"

"You don't like football. Yeah, I know. But that's because you don't know anything about it. And that's what makes it perfect. I mean, I'm assuming Cousin Violet knows you don't like football."

"She knows," Bailey says grimly. "Violet was a cheerleader."

Right. Violet was a cheerleader.

"Ah. And you didn't go to the games. Well—"

"I went," Bailey says, even more grimly. "Attendance was mandatory. School spirit stuff. You know?"

Of course I know. Villainous Vi twirled her pompoms while my girl sat in the stands.

"Well, that's good."

"It is?"

"Of course." I look around, catch our waiter's eye and nod. He nods back and heads for our table with the check. "Violet hears you talking football with me and any possible doubts she might have about our relationship will go up in smoke."

"They will?"

I hand the waiter my credit card. He whisks it away.

"Of course. It's proof, if she needs it, that you and I are an item. That we're close. I've got you liking football. That's the kind of sacrifice a woman makes for a man she—a man she cares for."

Bailey blinks. "It is?"

"It absolutely is," I say firmly, even as I suddenly remember that my mom, who adores my dad, has never learned to like what he considers, same as me, THE American pastime.

The waiter returns my credit card.

"Thank you, sir."

I add a tip to the bill, scrawl my name, and I'm already on my feet. I pull back Bailey's chair even as she starts pushing back from the table.

"Your date's job," I say.

She nods. "Got it."

I smile, ask the waiter to thank James for us, and we head into the night.

It's chilly. Bailey's new scarf isn't enough. I take off my tweed jacket and wrap it around her.

"Oh," she says, "you don't have to—"

But I do. For starters, it's the right thing. Besides that, I get a kick out of how she looks in it. She's so small and I'm so big. Even with her wearing those heels I'm taller than she is by six, seven inches. The result is that she's lost in my jacket and, damned if I know why, seeing her looking so delicately female in something that I know is still warm from my body is...

Christ!

I put my hand lightly in the small of her back and we head for the curb where I hail a taxi. We get in, and I give the driver my address.

"Isn't that your place?" Bailey says.

"It is."

"Why are we going there?"

"I've seen your apartment. Now you have to see mine so you can talk about it with some authority."

"If the subject should come up," she says.

"If it should," I say in agreement. "Plus, you get to meet Walter so you can talk about him too."

She thinks about that. "I guess that makes sense."

"And," I say, "so we can watch a football game."

She swings towards me. "Watch a what?"

I grin. "I tape the Monday night games so I can watch them whenever I have the chance. And this past Monday was an exceptional game."

"Because?"

"Because the Patriots played the Bills. In Buffalo."

"And the Patriots won?"

"Damn right."

"So if you already know that, why watch a boring game?"

"Boring?" I chuckle. "How little you know, woman," I say, and mostly because I can't help it, I lean close and kiss her gently on the mouth.

WALTER GREETS me the way he always does. I know it looks as if he's going to devour me whole, but his enthusiasm is slightly lessened by the presence of a new person in his life.

He takes his massive paws off my shoulders, drops to all fours and cocks his head at Bailey.

"He won't hurt you," I start to say, but my PA is already squatting down, holding out her hand and crooning *Who's a beautiful boy?* to my behemoth.

He approaches her slowly.

He doesn't see that many strangers. The truth is, I can't remember the last time I had someone here he didn't already know. See, the thing is, the guys I hang out with stop by for—what else?—football and occasional let's-just-bullshit sessions, but I don't make a habit of bringing women home with me.

Why would I?

It's easier to go to a woman's place after a night out. If I'm going to sleep with her, I don't really want to *sleep* with her. I want to fuck her. Too blunt for you? Maybe, but that's one of the things about guys. We're honest. We like sex. Remember when I said that before? Oh, sure, I'm into seduction, touching, kissing. I'm into holding a woman after sex. I don't run out. Hell, I'm not a boor. But unless I take a babe away for the weekend—admittedly, a rare occurrence—I almost always end the night by going home to my own bed.

I have Walter to take care of.

Plus, why put wrong ideas in a woman's head?

My space is my space, and I like to keep it that way.

So Walter's not the only guy here who's surprised to find a woman present. Truth is, he's

more than surprised.

He's making an ass of himself.

He's on his back, all four legs in the air, drooling and making little woofing sounds as Bailey kneels next to him, rubbing his belly.

Man, I'd drool and woof too, if she were rubbing mine.

I clear my throat.

"So," I say briskly, "how about some coffee? I mean, how about some tea? I don't have the white stuff, but—"

Bailey looks up, her face all smiles. "What a great dog Walter is!"

"Yeah. He's okay."

"Oh, he's wonderful!"

Walter moans with pleasure. Bailey laughs, rubs his belly a little more and says, "Don't you have to walk him?"

Walk. The doggy version of a sexy four-letter word. Walter springs to his feet, laps Bailey's face with his monstrous tongue, then turns his attention to me and jams his head into my balls.

"Sure," I say. "I'll just let him out into the garden..."

"I bet he would rather walk," Bailey croons. "Isn't that right, you big, beautiful boy?"

She's calling him sweet, intimate names—and I had to convince her to call me Matthew. I narrow my eyes at Walter as if this is all his fault.

Then I grab his lead and snap it to his collar.

Walter heads for the door. So does Bailey. Well, that's something. She's going to walk with us.

We make a circuit of the block. When we reach the corner, I start to turn back.

"It's such a nice night," Bailey says. "Can we walk a little further?"

"Well, sure. If that's what you want."

"Plus," she adds with a little giggle, "I'm starting to get used to these heels."

Yeah. So am I. I love the way the heels have changed her walk. Not that there was anything wrong with it before...But there's definitely something about really, really high heels that makes a woman's walk sexy.

We do the next block. And the next. We're so busy talking that I don't even realize that time is passing. As for Walter—he's in doggie heaven and he leaves no tree, no fire hydrant un-watered. Every now and then he looks up at Bailey and I could swear he smiles.

I don't blame him. I'm smiling too. At our conversation. We're just passing the time, but it's fun. Bailey comments on the wonderful old houses we pass. She admires the little shops. There's one on the corner that stops her dead. It's a bookshop, closed at this hour, of course, and there's a display of signed first editions in the window.

"*Fahrenheit 451*," Bailey says, her voice full of awe. "And *Peter Pan*! And, oh my, *Green Mansions*!"

I tell her that I never heard of *Green Mansions* and she gives me a quick rundown on the story of a sophisticated man who falls in love with a woman who is a creature of the rainforest. She makes the story sound exciting and beautiful, but what's really exciting and beautiful is the way she keeps looking up at me, all that intensity directed at me and only me...

"Time to head back," I say briskly.

A car suddenly speeds towards us as we step off the curb. I automatically grab Bailey's wrist.

"Careful," I say.

Somehow, our fingers entwine. They stay linked all the way back to my door.

Where she stops.

"It's late," she says.

I check my watch. "It's midnight."

"Exactly. It's late. And tomorrow's a work day."

"I know the boss. He won't mind if you come in late."

She raises one eyebrow. "I know him too. And he's a guy who believes in punctuality. It's time I went home."

She's right. Not about punctuality. Well, yeah. I do believe in it, but I don't want the evening to end. I don't want her to leave...

Meaning, it's time she did.

"Okay," I say, with a little smile. "Let me get Walter set and then I'll drive you home."

She shakes her head. "I can take the subway."

Spoken like a true New Yorker, but no way am I about to let her ride the subway at this hour. New York's a civilized city, sure, but there are times not all its citizens remember that.

"No subway," I tell her, and she makes a face.

"That's foolish."

"So is tempting the fates on the E train at this hour."

"Fine. I'll take a taxi and—"

"I'm driving you home." She starts to argue. I put my index finger against her lips. "Uh uh. No arguing with the boss."

She sighs and I unlock the door, undo Walter's lead, get him a couple of biscuits while Bailey hugs him and plants a kiss on his enormous muzzle.

Then she and I head for the door in the kitchen that leads to the garage.

Did I mention that it's a tight space?

She goes first and, being Bailey and being self-suffi-cient, she doesn't wait for me to open the door. She reaches for the doorknob herself. The problem is that me being me, I reach for it at virtually the same instant.

Meaning that we both end up in the same six inches of space.

"Sorry," I say.

"Sorry," she says.

She steps back.

Bad idea.

Awful idea.

Jesus.

It's a wonderful idea, because it puts her back against my front.

My dick against her ass. Her sweet, round ass.

So now it's my turn to step away. I know that. And it's what I intend to do—but somehow, some way, I close the last millimeter of space between us instead

And Bailey—Bailey is turning towards me, lifting her face to me.

I dip my head. Just a little. I don't kiss her. I just dip my head and her eyes widen and I slip my hand over her cheek, over her jaw, and then I gently run my thumb over her mouth.

I bend closer and now I can smell her.

She smells like lemons.

No. Like flowers.

I don't know much about flowers, but I think of the delicacy of the scent of the wildflowers that grow on that piece of hilly land I walked today.

That's what Bailey smells like.

Okay. Enough. I really will step back this time— but she's swaying towards me.

It's the shoes. It has to be the shoes. I'll steady her by clasping her waist.

Her hips.

Better still, I'll steady her by making sure she's leaning on me all the way, God, all the way, and she is. She's damn near plastered against me and I shift my weight and now there's not any space between us at all, and it's only logical that I slowly, slowly lower my head to hers. I can see that her eyes are half-shut, that her lips are slightly parted, and the next thing I know, my mouth is on hers.

Somebody groans. Is it me? It must be, because somebody else is making a sound that can only be described as a little moan—and that somebody is Bailey.

"Matthew," she says in a broken whisper.

"Hush," I tell her, and her hands rise, slip up my chest to my shoulders, and either I lift her into me or she raises herself into me, and when I kiss her this time, I don't hold back.

I kiss her hard and deep.

And I am lost.

Her taste fills me.

Sugar. Cream. Strawberries. She's the dessert we had a couple of hours ago, only twice as sweet, as smooth, as delicious.

You know those books where they talk about the earth shifting under your feet? No, I don't read that stuff but my sister does, always did, and okay, maybe I took a peek at a couple of those books when we were in our teens and...

And, the point is, the earth shifts.

There's never been a kiss like this before. I'm certain of it. It's a kiss that starts off honeyed and then goes hot, but the honeyed taste is still there, still amazing, and I want more.

Bailey gives me more.

Her arms go around my neck.

She moves against me.

I press her back against the door.

I keep kissing her. She moans again and her jacket —*my* jacket—slips back on her shoulders, baring her lovely throat, the rise of her breasts.

I slip the tip of my tongue between her lips, and she shudders and sucks on it.

Light explodes behind my closed eyelids.

My hands lift.

I cup her breasts.

I can feel the heat of her skin through the dress.

She makes a soft little sobbing sound and the earth doesn't just tilt. It spins.

And I am lost.

I want her. Here. Now. Against the door, her panties down around her ankles, my hands on her ass, her legs wound around my waist. I'll make her come and come and come, and then I'll scoop her up, carry her through the dark house to my bedroom, to my bed, to my possession...

Jesus H. Christ!

What the fuck am I doing?

This is Bailey. My PA. I'm with her tonight because I volunteered to help her get through the weekend ahead. I mean, this is all make-believe. It's a charade. A game. None of it is real; none of it is supposed to be real...

She seems to come to that identical realization at the same moment I do.

Suddenly, her hands are on my chest. She's

pushing me away and, okay, I'm complying, I'm step-ping back, putting some room between us, and then I clear my throat and I hear myself say, "Good. Very good. If we can pull off a kiss like that with Cousin Vi watching, you'll score an A for the weekend."

Bailey is breathing hard. Yeah, well, so am I. Her face is pink; her hair is disheveled. Her lipstick is all kissed away. She has the look of a woman who's just stepped from her lover's bed, and I get an instant mental picture of the bed, my bed, just one flight of stairs away...

"Is that why you..." Her voice is rusty. She takes a breath. "That's why you—it's why you and I—"

"Of course." I force a smile. "I probably should have warned you first, but I, ah, I figured a natural approach would make for a more natural reaction because, you know, we'll have to exhibit some affection this weekend if we expect to sell us as a package..."

I'm babbling.

I know it. I can only hope Bailey doesn't know it.

At this point, I'm not sure what she knows because my brain is still in free-fall, but I keep talking and talking and after a while she nods and her breathing steadies and I figure it's time to shut the hell up, get her into the garage, into the car, and out of my reach.

In other words, we need to get back to business— which is exactly what we do.

And when we get to her house, though she assures me it's unnecessary, I pull into a space next to a hydrant, walk her upstairs, take her keys from her, unlock the door like any proper gentleman would.

Then I shake hands with her, flash a smile and tell her I'll see her in the morning.

After which I drive home, strip off my clothes...and take a shower so cold I figure it's liable to turn my balls blue.

That solves the problem physically. But not mentally.

Because I end up spending most of the night tossing and turning, reliving the incredible feel of Bailey's mouth under mine.

9

I t starts raining at six a.m.

I know this because after finally getting a couple of hours of sleep, I am wide-awake at six.

I lie there for a couple of minutes. Then I toss back the covers and swing my feet to the floor. I need to do something. Something mindless that will burn up the energy buzzing inside me.

A run would do it—did I mention that I run three or four mornings a week? Normally, I pass if it's raining hard. And it is raining hard; there's a skylight over my bed and I can see and hear the rain hitting it.

Hell.

What's a little rain?

I get up, pull on sweats, running shoes, let Walter out into the garden to do his thing. The dog is smarter than I am. He gets back into the house fast, shakes off a ton of water even as I dry him with an enormous towel. Then I go into the soggy, grey morning. I don't last my usual five miles—I'm not a complete idiot—

but a couple of miles are enough to restore my equilibrium.

A hot shower, a couple of mugs of coffee, and I am calm and composed by the time I get to work.

I don't even think about that kiss. It was an aberration, and it's not going to happen again. Really, why would it? I've made my point. Impossible as it seems, Bailey and I can generate heat together. Well, sparks. Because surely my imagination has exaggerated the heat of that kiss. The point is, we'll be able to exchange a couple of light touches, light kisses in front of an audience and make the touches and the kisses seem real.

I'm hoping Bailey has come to the same conclusion. That she's figured out nothing spectacular happened in the doorway last night—and as soon as I step through the door, I can tell that's what she's done.

"Good morning, Mr. O'Malley," she say politely.

I nod. "Morning," I answer.

We start down the hall with her clipping along beside me, filling me in on a phone call that just came in from one of our suppliers. She's wearing one of those sexless suits; her shoes are sturdy; her hair is yanked back in a no-nonsense knot. She's completely businesslike; her tone is professional.

Excellent.

Life is back to normal. I was...well, not worried. Concerned, is the better word. I was concerned she'd have a difficult time forgetting that kiss. I mean, it's one thing for me to see it for the dress rehearsal it was. Hey, I'm an experienced dude. But Bailey's new to the game.

And she melted in my arms just a handful of hours ago.

Now, that same woman is briskly lining up a stack of memos on my desk.

There's not a hint of Bailey-From-Last-Night about her.

Okay. Maybe there is. She smells the same. As she leans over me, the scent of lemons and flowers drifts on the air. Is it from the tea she uses? Would white tea smell lemony?

"What's that smell?" I say. Actually, I blurt it. If I never quite got the meaning of that word, I get it now. The words shoot from my mouth before my brain can stop them.

She straightens up and looks at me. "What smell?"

"That scent. Lemon. And some kind of flower. Is it the tea you told me about?"

"The...Oh. Oh, no." She blushes. "It's lemon verbena. An herb. I use it."

"Oh. Got it." I look back at the memos. Then I look at her again. "As what?"

"As a lotion." Her blush deepens. "If the scent bothers you..."

"No," I say quickly, "it doesn't bother me at all. I just —I just wondered what...You use it as hand lotion, you mean? Or, you know, as a body lotion. Something you put on all over your skin..."

I clamp my mouth shut, look back at the memos.

"Where's my coffee?" I say—only I don't say it, I bark it.

Bailey rushes out of my office at which point I

groan, plant my elbows on my desk and put my face in my hands.

Didn't I just tell myself I'd exaggerated the memory of that kiss? I'm back in the real world. So how come that simple word, lotion, is ricocheting inside my skull like a table tennis ball set loose in a closet? How come my mind fills with a picture of Bailey, naked, while I smooth the stuff all over her? How come, despite what I've told myself, I can't forget that kiss?

Never mind those *how comes*.

The *how come* I'm interested in is how come her head isn't back in that kiss too?

Okay. What I need is to settle into work. I have plans to go over, meetings to arrange, orders to place. I start leafing through the memos; Bailey hurries in with my coffee. I manage to mutter a gruff thank you.

"Sir?"

I look up. "Will you please stop calling me that?"

"Sir," she says pointedly, "about the weekend..."

Aha. Here it comes. One kiss, and she's backing out of our arrangement. I push my chair back a little.

"Look, that kiss didn't mean a thing. I already explained..."

"I need to make plans."

"Bailey. If you want me to promise it won't happen ag—"

"Will you want to drive up?"

I blink. "Drive up where?"

"To Schenectady."

"Drive up to...Oh. To the wedding. I thought..." I clear my throat. "Sure. We'll drive."

She nods. "I just wanted to double check. I mean, there are choices. We could take the train. Or fly. Or—"

"We'll drive."

"Fine." She hesitates. Color begins sweeping into her face. "And what about lodging?"

"Lodging?"

"If my mother still had the house, we would stay there. But her condo is small. Smallish. There's a tiny den with a pullout sofa that she got second-hand. Well, third-hand. It was my Aunt Rose's and then Aunt Rose gave it to her daughter Thelma and when her daughter got married, she passed it along to my mother..." Bailey clamps her lips together, inhales, and starts fresh. "So I'd have to sleep with my mother. You'd have to sleep on the pullout sofa. But I can't, and neither can you."

I am getting lost in the syntax, meaning the safest response is, "Because?"

She shrugs. "Until three days ago, my mother didn't know I was going to the wedding. So she told my Aunt Sylvia that she and her husband could stay with her. Arthur—that's Aunt Sylvia's husband—is...he's a little heavy. He'll need the pullout sofa all to himself and Aunt Sylvia will sleep with my mother. When I phoned my mother and told her I was coming—that *we* were coming—she called my Aunt Cynthia to see if she could put up Sylvia and Arthur, instead, but—"

I hold up my hand. I am drowning in a sea of relatives I haven't even met.

"Book us into a hotel."

"Yes. I tried."

"But?"

"But, everything is filled." She looks at me. "There's some kind of renewable energy conference going on. Plus weddings. Not just Violet's. There are three others."

"Yeah, I get it, but there must be a room somewhere."

She nods. "I'll give it another try."

She plans my business trips with care. By late morning, I know she's planning this trip with the same concentration to detail.

She messages me, tells me she's contacted the woman who always takes care of Walter when I'm away. Mrs. Lopez will spend the weekend at my house and Walter will be happy. He adores her and she adores him.

"What about Prudence?"

"Prudence?"

"Your cat."

"Her name is Priscilla. Thank you for thinking of her."

What she means is, how are we going to pull this off if you can't even remember my cat's name?

"Mrs. Powell, across the hall from me, will stop in and take care of her."

"Great. Anything else?"

The tiniest pause. Then she says no, there's nothing else.

A little while later, she sends me a second message, informing me that she's checked the driving time from Manhattan to Schenectady. It's two hours and forty-nine minutes.

Not 2 hrs and 50 minutes? I text back.

Bailey ignores my feeble attempt at humor.

Two hours and forty-nine minutes. And we'll be travelling on a Friday, so it might take longer.

Is there a specific time... I stop typing, shake my head, get to my feet, go out of my office and walk the five feet to her desk. "Is there a specific time we have to be there?" I ask.

She looks up at me. "There's a rehearsal dinner at six."

"Fine. I'll pick you up at two. That'll give us time to allow for traffic."

"Yessir."

I narrow my eyes. "You need to get used to calling me Matthew."

"Yes. I will." She wants to get rid of me. I can feel it. "Was there anything else?"

"No. Yes. What else is on the weekend's agenda? The rehearsal dinner. And the wedding... Is that Saturday day or evening?"

"It's Saturday evening."

"Black tie? White?"

"Oh. Sorry. I should have told you. It's black tie."

"No problem. Just as long as it isn't Bermudas, socks, oxfords, and no shirt. Anything else?"

All of a sudden, a little furrow appears between her eyebrows.

"Problem?" I say.

"Just a couple of details."

"Details?"

"Yes. I'll work them out."

"Because if there's anything I can do to help..."

"You can give me some space," she snaps. She looks horror-stricken. "Oh my God, Mr. O'Malley! I didn't mean to—"

I hold up my hands and step back. "I'm here if you need me," I tell her, and I try not to smile until I'm safely in my office.

My girl is going to do just fine this weekend.

In fact, Venal Vi probably won't know what hit her.

A WHILE LATER, the intercom buzzes. I hit the play button.

"Look, if you're worrying about what happened before—"

"We have a problem," Bailey says.

At least, I think that's what she says because she's whispering into the intercom.

"What problem? Don't tell me those teak doors..."

"The Colonial Inn," she hisses.

"What colonial inn?"

"*The* Colonial Inn!"

I roll my eyes. "Bailey. How about coming into my office and talking to me?"

The intercom goes silent. A second later, my door opens. Bailey steps into the room. She's obviously upset.

"What's going on?"

She shuts the door, walks to my desk, stands staring at me.

"I found lodging for us. A suite. At a place called The Colonial Inn. But—"

"But what?"

"It's not a regular suite."

"Then what is it?"

"I mean, they call it a suite. But I checked online. They have a photo of it."

"Listen, I don't care if it's too big, if it's a copy of Versailles, if it has, I don't know, half a dozen bedrooms and half a dozen bathrooms, a game room and a grand piano and...Dammit, woman! What now?"

"When they say *suite* what they really mean is a bedroom with a pullout sofa."

"And?"

"Did you not hear me? It's just one room."

"With a pullout sofa. So what's the problem?"

There's a silence. Bailey looks unhappy. She looks down. Looks up. Looks down...

"Bailey. What's going on?"

"Schenectady is a small town. I mean, it's a city, but in many ways..." She swallows. "The desk clerk turns out to be a guy I went to school with."

"And?"

"And," she says in a rush, "once I book that room everybody will know we're sleeping together." She turns a bright shade of red. "I mean, they'll think we're sleeping together. And—and—"

I push back my chair and rise to my feet. "No problem. I'll leave the pullout sofa open. The chambermaid will realize we're not sharing the bed."

"Yes. I thought of that. But if we do—if we do that, she'll spread the word that we're not actually a couple. And we're supposed to be a couple."

"Okay. I'll close the sofa each morning. How's that?"

Not good either. I can tell by the way she's looking at me. She inhales. Exhales. Then she says, "The thing is, I've never—I've never shared a room with a man before."

"Well, that's no prob..." Wait. What does that mean? That she's never shared a room with a man? Or she's never shared a bed? She can't be talking about sex. No way. Never having had a boyfriend doesn't mean she's never had sex.

The possibility flashes through me like a shot of electricity, but I simply nod my head.

"Well," I say solemnly, "there are benefits. To sharing with a guy, I mean. For instance, you won't have to worry about me hogging the bathroom so I can put on my makeup."

She blinks. And gives me a tiny, barely there smile. I smile in return.

"It'll be fine," I tell her. "And Venal Violet—" Bailey laughs, which is even better than that quick smile. "Venal Vi will never torment you again. Okay?"

"Okay," she says, and I come around the desk and

clasp her shoulders. I give them a reassuring squeeze. What I want to do is nuzzle her hair aside and drop a kiss on her neck. Nothing major. Just a little kiss, but I don't because there's no reason for it.

Well, yeah. There is.

The reason is that I want to taste her, breathe her in. And that's out of the question. I mean, how can I promise her that everything will be cool when we share a bedroom if I can't keep from wanting to kiss her when we're just standing here in my office?

So I turn the shoulder squeeze into the kind of casual thing a guy would give his sister and then I move away.

"Okay," I say briskly. "What else do we have to do?"

"We'll need a gift. I'll pick up something when I go to the mall during my lunch hour."

"Forget that. Just phone Tiffany's and send the happy couple something big and expensive and, if we're lucky, ostentatious."

Bailey hesitates. "I don't think I can really afford—"

"It's on me. Hey, I haven't had this much fun since the day I stole Mindy Cassini's gym shorts and ran 'em up the school flagpole."

This time, Bailey giggles. "You stole some girl's gym shorts?"

"It was a long time ago," I say, and I wonder why I'd think back to something that happened all those years before. "So. What else?"

"Nothing else." She hesitates. "Well, there's maybe one little thing..."

"Yes?"

"Is it all right if I take lunch little early? Or maybe skip my lunch break and leave at four instead of five?"

The only other time she asked to leave early was a couple of years ago when it turned out she'd come down with the flu. I frown and check her out. She looks fine. Or, yeah, maybe she looks a little flushed.

"Are you okay?"

"Yes."

"You sure?"

"I am positive," she says in a no-nonsense tone, but she's definitely flushed.

"Listen, if you're feeling sick—"

"I have to go shopping! Shopping, Mr. O'Malley! Must I explain everything to you?"

"Whoa. If you want to go shopping—"

"I did not say I *want* to, I said I *have* to."

"I don't get the difference. And how come we're back to 'Mister'? I thought we settled..." Then it hits me. "Shopping," I say slowly. "To get something to wear to the wedding."

"The wedding. The rehearsal dinner. Friday day. Saturday day. Sunday day..."

She's standing with her chin up, her eyes bright, her hands on her hips. She's looking defiant, but I'm pretty sure I can see past that to what she's really feeling.

Fear.

Fear of the unknown. I've see that look before, on my man Cooper's face right before he stepped out of a plan for his first skydive. Remember Cooper? My best pal through middle school, high school, college, heck, through life? We've been tight forever—and he'd have seen that look on my face if he hadn't gone out the door of the plane before I did.

This isn't skydiving, but it's just as bad. Bailey's about to walk into a glitzy store, face a judgmental clerk, and be presented with endless, terrifying choices.

"Right," she says briskly, "so I'm taking a long lunch."

"Yes. Of course. Take the rest of the day."

"Thank you."

I nod. She heads for the door. Or maybe for disaster.

This cannot possibly go well. And I can't help her. I mean, I could say I'll go with her, but what good would that be? Last night only worked because we picked up shoes, a purse, a scarf. Small, easy-to-choose stuff. This is different. This will be a shopping expedition, not a shopping trip.

Besides, if I were picking out her clothes, I'd stop at a white lace bra and panties. Okay, maybe throw in a pair of shoes. One of the spike heeled jobs we got last night. And for a little variety, something short and silky, something that would cling to her breasts and her hips and...

Goddammit.

She needs a woman to shop with her.

Think, I tell myself. Think! There has to be a solution.

A couple of possibilities come to mind, but none is good.

I could phone one of the women I've dated. Explain that Bailey is a business associate. Explain that she needs some help choosing a weekend's worth of clothes and, whoops, did I forget to mention that she needs them for a weekend in the country with me?

I shove back my chair, get to my feet and start pacing.

No. Not a good plan. Not a good plan at all.

Possibility number two.

Pick a store. Call and ask to speak with a personal shopper. I know such people exist. I've seen the discreet signs pointing the way to their offices. Offer the lady the same lame explanation, the business associate thing, blah blah blah. A personal shopper's no more likely to fall for it than an ex-girlfriend, but who cares?

Bailey. That's who would care. No matter how helpful a personal shopper would be, Bailey would not feel comfortable.

There's only one thing that will work.

I whip out my cellphone and hit a button. My sister answers on the first ring.

"Hi," she says breathlessly. "Look, if Jenny's had a problem with the Phillips kid again, I'm sorry. But, really, somebody needs to tell him that he cannot go around deliberately finger-painting other kids and..." She pauses. "Matt? Is that you?"

"That's one of the amazing things about smart-phones, Case. All you have to do is look at the screen and you can see who's calling."

Casey gives a deep sigh. "I know. But Jenny's preschool called this same time yesterday and the day before, and I just figured—"

"So what happens when this juvenile delinquent finger-paints my niece? If the little so-and-so makes her cry—"

"Only the first time. Now she marches straight to the water colors, grabs a container and dumps it over his head."

I laugh.

"Don't laugh, Matt. It isn't..." That's as far as she gets before she laughs too. "Welcome to my world, brother dearest—and hold on a sec while I wipe up some puppy pee."

I wait while my sister does her thing. She leads a busy life. A big house. A toddler. A puppy. A husband who owns a technology company. And she loves it all, wants it all, and not even the husband she adores and who adores her can figure out how she manages to deal with everything while still running her online business, *Casey's Quest*. Yeah. She's that Casey, the one whose site helps busy women locate stuff like antique perfume bottles and antimacassars, not that I really know what in hell an antimacassar is or why anybody would want to locate one.

"Okay," she says. "I'm back. Hey. Is everything okay? You don't usually phone me during the day."

"Everything is fine." I run my hand through my hair. "I just, uh, I just need a little advice."

She laughs again. "On what? Potty training? Puppy train—Mongo! Mongo, put down that slipper. Bad puppy. Baaad puppy!"

"Mongo? You named a two month old Golden Retriever Mongo?"

"Talk to your brother-in-law. He's seen *Blazing Saddles* more times than any human being should."

Now I'm the one who's laughing. It almost—*almost*—makes it a little easier to get to the reason for my call.

"Case?"

"Mmm?"

"That advice I need...It's more like a favor. You got a couple of free hours today?"

My sister doesn't just laugh, she guffaws.

"I guess not," I say glumly.

"At least tell me what the favor is. Who knows? Maybe today's when I figure out how to turn twenty-four hours into twenty-five."

"It's a favor for my Bailey."

"Bailey? The woman who should get the *Croix de Guerre* for putting up with you all these years?"

"See, she's got this wedding to go to," I say, ignoring the comment. "A family thing. It's a three day job, Friday through Sunday."

"Three days in the bosom of her family? Wow. I hope she doesn't have an Uncle Harry."

Uncle Harry is a man whose views on virtually anything you might foolishly mention are enough to empty a room.

"Close enough. She has a Cousin Violet."

"Ah."

"Violet's the sort who pulls wings off flies. And if

Bailey doesn't show up looking like a fashion plate, she'll end up being the fly."

"Poor Bailey. I admit, she doesn't exactly, you know, wear the things she should. I mean, if she did, she'd be a knockout because, basically, she's a really pretty girl."

"You see that too?"

"What do you mean, do I see that too? Who's the 'too' in this equation?"

I close my eyes. I am absolutely not taking the conversation in that direction.

"What I mean is, you have an excellent eye. And you always look great."

"Puppy pee and baby drool will do that," my sister says. "So forget the compliments and get to the favor. What is it you need from me?"

"I need you to take her shopping."

"Bailey?"

"Yes."

"To buy some clothes for this wedding?"

"Right."

"How does she feel about that? Shopping is a personal kind of thing."

"I see packs of women in stores all the time."

"What you see are friends," my sister says, a little coldly, "not packs. And they're just bonding."

"Whatever. The question is, are you willing to do it?"

I feel a tug at my sleeve. I pivot and there's Bailey, staring at me and shaking her head frantically from side to side.

"Take Bailey shopping?"

"Yes." I glare at Bailey. "Take Bailey shopping."

More head-shaking. I turn away. No good. Bailey turns with me.

"When?" Casey asks.

"Today."

"The wedding is this weekend?"

"Right." Bailey digs her fingers into my arm. I mouth *Stop that!* and shake free. "I know it's last minute, but—"

"I'd have to leave all this pee-and-poop behind, bribe Mongo with a butterscotch cookie so I can corral him into his crate, ask Liam to leave work early so he can pick up Jenny..."

"Yeah. Right. I understand. I should have figured—"

"Where am I meeting Bailey and when?"

"You mean you'll do it?"

Casey gives a very unladylike snort. It's a nice counterpoint to the punches I'm taking in the biceps. Turns out Bailey has a pretty good right.

"Of course. I love Bailey. If she needs me, she's got me. Just give me ten minutes to shower and change into something that won't make people scream and run."

"Where?"

Bailey is shaking her head from side to side the way Walter did this morning, after he came in from the rain.

Casey names a mall maybe twenty minutes from my office.

"It's upscale," she tells me. "Lots of good stores.

Small ones. Big ones. We can find everything we...Uh oh."

"Uh oh, what?"

"This is going to be an expensive afternoon, Matt. I'm sure you pay Bailey well, but...Maybe you'd better ask her to give me some parameters."

Expensive. I think back to last night. The shoes. The purse. The scarf. Yup. This trip is gonna be pricey, and way outside what even a well-paid PA can afford.

"Don't worry about cost," I say briskly. "It's on me. Her annual bonus—ouch!"

Bailey's glare is as hard as her punch. I grab her wrist. She starts to come at me with her other hand so I drop the phone and grab it too.

She's furious. Fiery with anger. I haul her closer and she loses her footing and tumbles against me. For a heartbeat, her body is pressed to mine and I flash back to last night, that doorway, that kiss...

"Matt? Did I lose you?"

I swallow hard, let go of my PA, and scramble for the phone on the floor.

"Thirty minutes," I say briskly.

"Make it forty-five," my sister says. "Tell Bailey I'll meet her at the main entrance to Nordstrom's."

"Will do," I say, but it's a lie.

I don't have to tell Bailey anything. Considering how things just went, I'll have to go on this little trip with her.

∾

SHE SITS AS FAR from me as she can in the 'Vette. She's not just angry, she's totally pissed off.

"You had no right to involve your sister in this," she says coldly.

"You *involve* people in conspiracies," I say, trying to lighten the mood. "This is a simple shopping trip."

"There's nothing simple about your sister knowing that we're going to—that we're going to—"

"Spend the weekend in a suite-that's-not-really-a-suite together?"

Okay. The look she shoots me makes it clear bad jokes are not the way to improve her mood.

"Look," I say, "all Casey knows is that you're going to a family thing and you want to knock their eyes out."

Another look that could kill. "I am not that kind of person," Bailey says," nor do I wish to become one."

Nor do I wish to become one. I can almost hear my Mom applauding.

"And you're leaving out the fact that you're going to the wedding with me so you can pretend to be my—my lover."

She says the word as if it's a synonym for leper. I want to laugh, but sanity prevails.

"Casey doesn't have to know anything about that." I shift a little behind the wheel. Truth is, I don't want my sister to know the full plan. There'd be too many questions and raised eyebrows and jokes and speculation when there's nothing to speculate about. "All she needs are the basics. You're going to a family function you don't really want to go to, and you want to make the whole crew sit up and take notice."

"Not everybody. Just my cousin."

"Venomous Vi."

If I hoped for a laugh, I don't get one. All I get is a *hmpf* and a narrow-eyed glare.

"And how do I explain your presence today?"

"You don't. I'll just say I'm along for the ride."

"And why, exactly—just for my own information—are you insisting on going with me?"

"You'll hold back on what you spend if I'm not there," I tell her bluntly. "And we cannot let that happen."

"*We* cannot?"

"That's right. We. As in, I'm in this with you. Because I volunteered. I wasn't shanghaied or coerced."

"What you mean is, you're my boss. And you think that gives you the right to make the rules."

I don't hesitate. All you feminists out there, take a breath because you're not going to like my answer.

"Yes," I say. "It does."

10

My sister is right where she said she'd be, standing outside the main entrance to Nordstrom's. She looks a little surprised to see me, but she doesn't say that. Instead, she says 'Hi' to Bailey, gives her a quick hug and then does the same for me.

"Thank you for doing this," Bailey says, in pretty much the same way you'd thank your dentist for skipping the Novocain and going straight in with the drill. "I told Mr. O'Malley he shouldn't have bothered you, but—"

"It's no bother at all." Casey smiles. "In fact, I'm delighted to spend a few hours doing girl stuff." She looks at me. "No reason to wait here, Matt. I can run Bailey back to the office when we're done."

"No problem," I say. "I'm going to tag along with you."

Casey stares at me. "You are?"

I shrug my shoulders as if to assure her that I do this kind of thing all the time.

"It's a quiet day at the office. I figured I'd join the party."

From the look my sister gives me, my answer sounds as lame to her as it sounds to me. In fact, I can almost see her filing it away so she can pull it out later and try to make sense of it.

"Mr. O'Malley doesn't trust me to spend his money wisely," Bailey says.

"Your money. Not mine. Your bonus money. And would you do us both a favor and stop that 'Mr. O'Malley' crap?"

This time, Casey stares at both of us. Yeah. Okay. I shouldn't have said that—but how can a woman who burned in my arms not twelve hours ago go back to calling me Mr. O'Malley? Why would she be so damn intent on building a wall between us?

"Sorry," I mutter. "I guess I didn't get enough caffeine this morning."

Casey nods. Then she links arms with my PA and smiles.

"Okay," she says, her voice even brighter than her smile, "how about we get started? We have lots to do and not much time to do it in."

She heads into the store with Bailey marching beside her. I wait a couple of seconds before I fall in behind them.

And I remind myself that I am going to have to be exceedingly careful of what I say.

MAN, the things dudes don't know about women's clothing.

You're a guy, shopping is easy. Shirts? You go to the Shirt department. Tees? In the same place as shirts, except in their own little area. Pants are in—what else? —the Pants department. And right there you can locate khakis and jeans and what my Mom always calls trousers, the kind of pants you wear with a sports jacket. I could go on like this for a while—suits are in the Suit department, ties and socks are in the Accessories area—but you get my drift.

Men's clothing is sold in logical, easy-to-figure ways.

Women's stuff...You don't just need a map, you need a compass, a sextant, and a translator.

My sister has drawn up a list. She's come up with a plan. She's figured out what Bailey will need for a three-day weekend and she's prioritized it, meaning she's ranked things in their order of importance. So numero uno on this list is Something to Wear to the Saturday Night Wedding.

I think this means we're going to the dress department.

We're not.

Well, we are. Sort of. Where we go is to Evening Wear, and after a swift look through the racks, Casey shakes her head and we hunt down Cocktail Wear. Another rack check and we have to ferret out Separates. Not Sportswear Separates. Not Business Separates. Separates, as in long skirts and short ones, velvet pants and silk ones, tops that look like they're made out of gauze and others with enough beads to throw off your vision.

Nothing is right, Casey decides,

"I wanted to get Saturday night out of the way," she says, "but there are other shops in the mall for that, so let's just see if we can get some of the other things we need while we're still here. Something to wear Friday, for instance."

This turns out to mean that we're going to Sportswear and then narrow our search even further, from Sportswear to Designer. After some exploration, she determines which designer does clothes that will work best for Bailey. She accomplishes this even though, at first, it becomes a cross-examination.

"Patterns?" she asks. "Or solids?"

Bailey shrugs. "I'm not sure."

"Low slung pants or high waist?"

Another shrug.

"Favorite colors?"

"I don't have favorite colors."

I am sure she would show more enthusiasm in a dental chair.

"Black and anything that looks like black," I say. Both women look at me. I hold up my hand. "Sorry."

And I *am* sorry. I am in a bad mood. I've no idea why—or maybe I do. Maybe it's because I can see that my PA's heart isn't really in this. Is she seriously upset about the bonus thing? Should I have let her go shopping alone? Am I pushing her too hard? Is she regretting that she agreed to let me go with her this weekend?

Or is she sorry about that kiss last night?

Because I am not sorry. Okay. I am. But what I'm sorry about is that I didn't follow through, take it further because, hell, I wanted to, I still want to, and why isn't she feeling what I feel...

"...do you think?"

I am leaning against a pillar, arms folded over my chest, staring into space.

"Matt? What do you think?"

I blink and realize that Casey is looking at me.

"Sorry. What do I think about what?"

"About this outfit?" she says, and points to the right, so I turn in that direction and I see Bailey, standing outside the fitting room.

Bailey, in a white T with long sleeves and a V-neck. Bailey, in white pants that skim what are obviously long, long, incredible legs. Bailey, with her hair loose and hanging in soft waves. down her back...

"For tomorrow," Casey says into the silence. "The drive up to Schenectady. Add this blazer—" She holds out a jacket the color of a ripe apricot—"and a pair of white mules, and it's a perfect look."

"Perfect," I say, and to hell with why a woman would want mules on her feet. All I can see is my beautiful PA, her chin high, her cheeks the same shade as the jacket, and something inside me twists. "More than perfect."

"Great," my sister says.

And Bailey—

Bailey lets out a long breath.

And is that...?

It is.

It's a smile.

IT'S EASIER AFTER THAT.

The white outfit. The apricot blazer. A pair of white mules which turn out to be shoes without backs and I make a mental note to Google mules and find out why that's what they're called because there must be some kind of logic in this fantasyland called women's clothing.

Jeans. A couple of T-shirts. A pale blue dress. It's the same blue as the butterfly-wing shoes we got last night, and I can already picture Bailey in the dress with the shoes.

And Bailey's participating.

Turns out she has some definite ideas. Likes and dislikes. I begin to suspect that long-ago shopping trips with Vexatious Vi had left their mark, and now, with my sister's gentle guidance, those memories are fading.

I make two trips out to the parking lot to deposit bags and boxes in the car. When I rejoin my ladies, they're sitting on a bench, Starbucks containers in their hands. Casey's holding two; she hands me one.

"Black," my sister says. "Two sugars."

I nod. "Thanks."

"Don't thank me. Thank Bailey." She sighs. "Liam and I have been together six years and I'd bet he hasn't the foggiest idea of how I take my coffee. I guess working together day after day has made you guys pretty close."

Bailey and I look at each other. She blushes. I do the male equivalent, meaning I clear my throat.

Casey's eyebrows lift.

I try to come up with something clever to say. Then I decide the best thing is to say nothing, so I all but bury my face in my cup and drink my coffee. Bailey does the same and after looking from one of us to the other, Casey gives what I'm sure is a mental shrug and joins us.

After a while, we're all holding empty containers.

"Well," Casey says, "we've only got one thing left." She looks at Bailey. "Something for you to wear to the wedding. Any ideas?"

Bailey's been offering opinions for the past hour or so. This time, she shakes her head.

"None."

"Well, what kind of wedding is it going to be? Afternoon? Evening? The party, I mean. Small? Big? At home? In a hotel?"

Bailey sighs. "Evening. At a country club. My cousin is into, you know, glitz. And the invitation says Black Tie. Matthew said that means he'll have to wear a tu—"

An expression of sheer horror spreads over her face. She clamps her lips together, but it's too late. Casey's mouth is hanging open.

""My brother is going with you?"

Bailey looks at me. *Say something*, her eyes plead.

"Matt? You and Bailey are—"

"Bailey and I are in cahoots," I say quickly. "See, she didn't want to run the risk of being seated with this, ah, this guy. A friend of the, uh, the groom. Whenever she goes home to visit, he makes a move on her, so —so I offered to—to be her date and—and—"

Bailey reaches for my hand and squeezes it.

"Matthew is just trying to protect me," she says in a low voice. "To keep me from being embarrassed. The truth is that my cousin—the bride..." She takes a deep, deep breath. "We don't get along. We never have. And when she began planning this wedding she made a big thing out of how sorry she was that I'd be coming to it alone, that everyone else would be bringing someone and she wanted me to bring someone too, but she knew that there probably wasn't anyone—any man—I knew well enough to ask to go with me, so I lied and told my mother to say that the reason I wouldn't be going was that—that a rich, sexy guy was taking me away for that weekend and—and— Matthew—your brother—he heard about it and he offered to—to—"

It's my turn to squeeze Bailey's hand.

"I told Bailey she'd be doing me a favor if she let me escort her to the wedding because that way I'd have an excuse to spend a couple of days away from the city, breathing in clean country air."

Casey is staring at me. I can almost see the gears in her head whirring. When we were kids, she'd have listened to that last bit and laughed. But we're grownups now and, as I said, we're close. So even as those gears in her brain are still going one hundred miles an hour, she smiles, nods, turns to Bailey and says, "That's great. I keep telling him he needs a break and now he's finally going to take one."

Bailey exhales. Nods. We all sit there for another few seconds. Then Casey gets to her feet.

"Well," she says briskly, "let's get this show on the road. Evening wedding. Black tie." She flashes Bailey a big smile. "*Chateau d'Or*, here we come."

Bailey stares at my sister. "Really? The *Chateau d'Or*?"

Her tone is half awe, half delight. We head for the far end of the mall and when we get there, I understand her reaction. The *Chateau* is not so much a shop as it is an inner sanctum, all fresh flowers and soft music and gilt-framed mirrors.

But for all that, the saleswoman is low key and immediately puts Bailey at ease. I get waved to a handsome upholstered chair; Bailey gets sent into a fitting room.

Casey huddles with the saleswoman, who nods her head, says *Of course* and *Yes* and then hurries off through a curtained doorway.

My sister leans towards me.

"Is there anything you want to tell me?" she whispers.

"Not a thing," I whisper back.

"You're going away with a sweet, shy girl for three days and there's nothing you want to tell me?"

"She's a woman, not a girl. And I'm not going away with her. Not the way you mean. I'm her friend. This is strictly an act of friendship,"

"Friendship, huh? Three days at a wedding when we both know that weddings make you shudder?"

"The wedding won't last for three days. "

"You know what I mean."

"And they don't make me shudder. I'm just not, you know, into that kind of thing."

"Not just three days at a wedding. Three days in the country."

"What's wrong with the country?"

"Nothing, except it isn't Manhattan."

"I like the country."

"You like Central Park."

"Trees. Grass. Same thing."

My sister bends close enough so I'm almost cross-eyed as I try to focus on her face.

"If you hurt this girl," she says grimly, "I'll never forgive you."

"I told you, she's a woman, not a girl. And I have no intention of hurting her. I like her. I respect her. Didn't you hear what I said? This is strictly an act of friendship."

While we've been going at each other in whispers, the salesclerk has hustled past us with an armful of gowns. We haven't paid her any attention; we've been too busy squaring off. Now, there's a discreet cough.

"Pardon me."

Casey straightens up and turns around. The salesclerk smiles and holds back the dressing room curtain.

Bailey appears.

She's wearing a long, slender column of pale pink. Later, I learn the color is called blush, but pale pink is close enough. It leaves one shoulder exposed. One pale, lovely shoulder. The gown—silk, I think—clings to the curve of her breasts and embraces her waist; it skims her hips and legs like a lover's caress. She's wearing spiked heels the color of the gown and when she takes a step forward, I see that the gown is slit so that when she moves, you get a discreet but incredibly provocative glimpse of ankle, calf and thigh. Her hair is a loose, shiny fall of soft curls drawn away from her flushed face with silver combs.

Beside me, Casey breathes out one word. "Wow," she says, and brings her hands together in what might be either prayer or applause.

Bailey's eyes are wide. For a heartbeat, her lips curve upward, but the smile is hesitant and fades as she fixes her gaze on me.

"Matthew?" she says. "What do you think? It this all right?"

The correct response is to say yes, it's fine, we'll take it.

But I don't say anything.

What I do is rise to my feet, walk straight to her, cup her face in my hands and lower my mouth to hers.

11

We get out of the store, out of the mall. I do not make eye contact with Casey.

"Well," I say briskly, "it's getting late. Thanks, Case..."

"Thank you doesn't even come close," Bailey says, flinging her arms around my sister. The women hug.

Then it's my turn.

Casey lets go of Bailey, steps up to me and puts her arms around me. She rises up on her toes and puts her cheek against mine.

I'm sure it looks like a gesture of sibling love.

It isn't.

She puts her lips to my ear.

"Remember the time you were eight and I was ten?" she whispers. "You told Billy Hamilton I had a crush on him and I beat you up."

"Yes," I say brightly, "you were wonderful."

"I can still beat you up, bro. I do yoga. Pilates. Tai Chi. I can see to it that your ass is grass."

Carefully, smiling as if she said something vastly amusing, I clasp her shoulders and put her from me.

"Not on your best day."

She throws back her head and gives a big, phony laugh. "Oh, you're funny!" Then she leans in again. "I also took a self-defense class. They taught us that kneeing a guy in the balls can take him down real fast." This time, she pulls back without any help from me. She laughs again and pats my cheek. "So keep that in mind this weekend, okay?"

I tell her to kiss my niece for me, say hi to my brother-in-law, and I then I grasp Bailey's arm and hustle her away.

"What was that about?" she asks as we head for my car.

"Oh, just some sisterly advice." I dump the last armload of boxes into what passes for a rear seat in a Corvette—by now, it's jammed to the roof with stuff—and get behind the wheel.

"Advice?"

I nod, start the car, and back out of the parking space. "You know. Bread-and-butter plate is to the left, wine glass to the right, dessert fork's above the plate. Don't do anything to embarrass the family name. That kind of thing."

The deception works. Bailey smiles and says that if we end up seated with her Uncle Alan, none of that will matter because he'll grab the wrong plate, the wrong glass, the wrong fork and then everyone else will have no choice but to do the same thing.

"My kind of guy," I say, and we keep the banter

going all the way back to the office, where I pull in next to Bailey's car and we get out of the 'Vette so we can switch all the packages to her trunk.

Then we look at each other.

It's not a comfortable moment.

I feel pretty much as if I were fourteen, standing outside her door with the first girl I ever took on a date. Well, no. Not exactly. Back then, my Mom was waiting for me at the end of the driveway in her Chevy Malibu because she'd driven us back and forth to the movies, but I have that same sense of trying to figure what I'm supposed to do next.

Bailey breaks the vaguely uneasy silence.

"Matthew. I want to thank you for—"

"I'm glad to help."

"I'll repay you for all the things you bought."

"No way. I won't permit it. I came up with this idea; I'll see it through."

"I will," she said, with that tilt of her chin and that look of determination that make her the best PA you could ever want.

"Let's argue about it after we see if Uncle Al uses the right fork."

That wins me a smile. Such a soft, easy smile. It makes me want to lean down and kiss her again—but I am done with courting danger. This whole thing is, just as I'd told my sister, one friend doing something helpful for another friend. Nothing less. Nothing more.

Right.

Except doing something helpful for a friend isn't supposed to make you want to scoop that friend into your arms, carry her off to a quiet place where you can strip her naked and kiss her everywhere, touch her everywhere...

"Okay," Bailey says. "So, I'll see you in the office tomorrow."

"No. Forget that."

"We don't have to leave until the afternoon, remember?"

"Yeah. I know. But there's nothing on the calendar for tomorrow. I checked."

Another smile. "*You* checked?"

"I know. I never do. I rely on you. But I looked and we're clear all day tomorrow. So I'll just pick you up at your place at noon. Good?"

"You said two."

"That might be cutting it a little close. Noon, okay?"

"Fine. And, really, thank you."

"Hey," I say, "I'm the one who should be thanking you. Without today's little foray into Mall World—"

She laughs. "Mall World?"

"Without it, I'd never know the difference between Valentino and McQueen and all those other bozos."

Another smile. "Neither would I. Your sister is wonderful."

"Yeah. She's improved some since she was ten."

Smile number three, and damned if I don't want to take my PA in my arms and kiss her.

The realization terrifies me. That kiss in front of my sister. Now I've come within a second of a kiss in the parking lot where anybody who works for me could see us.

I did mention I used to play football, right? And soccer. Yeah, and I'm still fast on my feet. In a heartbeat, I'm around the side of my car and safe behind the wheel.

"See you tomorrow," I say.

Then I step on the gas and get the hell away from temptation.

Driving home is difficult. Not the drive itself. What's difficult is trying to get past those last sudden minutes of, I don't know, insanity. Wanting to kiss her again.

And again.

And...

I take a long breath, hold it for a count of five, and then slowly expel it. Doing eighty on the highway might not be the best place for Zen, but neither is realizing that something in what had looked like a simple plan has gone terribly wrong.

My brain feels scrambled.

Was it the hours spent learning the differences between petite, juniors, misses and women's sizes? Not even the positions in football are that confusing, but no, that stuff had all sorted out pretty fast.

Was it the total realization of what I'd volunteered to do? Playing a game of payback to get even with a woman who'd subjected my girl—sorry, my PA—to years of not-so-subtle torture? Nope. Payback's a bitch, and Vituperative Vi deserves everything she's gonna get.

Okay, Mr. Contestant. So if it's not Number One that made you run like a rabbit and it's not Number

Two, what is it? After all, the plan is set. The game is about to begin. I am ready and eager to start.

True.

But I'm also ready, eager and desperate to have my way with my girl. With my PA.

With my Bailey.

I frown. Have my way with who? With whom? Frankly, I don't give a crap whether it's who or whom. What matters is that Bailey is not *my* anything. Well, yeah. She's my PA. But the rest of it...

Jesus.

What I want to do is fuck her.

And that is definitely not part of the plan.

I could do it too. I'm no idiot. I know women. I know what it means when a woman slips into my arms, when she raises her face to mine, when she makes those soft little sounds as we kiss...

A horn blares. I spin the wheel to the right and it takes a long two seconds of sweat before I avoid ending up on the median, which is unthinkable. I am a good driver. Better than good. I've done some semi-pro racing—Corvettes are made for speed, after all—and I take pride in my never-had-an-accident-anywhere-anytime record. Which I came awfully close to breaking just now.

Carefully, I maneuver to the right lane. I take the next exit, pull over as soon as it's okay to do so, take out my iPhone and hit a speed dial button.

Cooper answers.

"What?"

Not a good sign. He sounds distracted. That gives

me two choices. He's either with a woman—Coop, like me, is no slouch when it comes to women—or he's just made some kind of scientific discovery that will undoubtedly win him the Nobel Prize.

I don't care.

I need his full attention, and whether he has to zip up his fly or his head doesn't matter.

"It's me."

"And?"

"Are you in the middle of something?"

"I'm almost in the middle of something. Speak, and make it fast."

"I have to talk to you."

"Call back in five minutes."

Despite everything, that makes me laugh. "Coop. My man. I'm disappointed. Better still, I'll bet the lady will be disappointed."

I hear a woman's voice. Coop answers, but his words are as muffled as hers.

"Five minutes," he says into the phone.

"Make it twenty, and meet me at The Attic."

"Done," Coop says, and disconnects.

THE ATTIC IS one of those places downtown that's halfway between a dive bar and a cocktail lounge. There's lots of time-worn mahogany, a string of leather booths, and the lighting is dim. Maybe because of its location, it draws a mixed crowd. Financial hotshots in dark suits, professorial types with leather patches on their jacket sleeves; guys who spent the day working heavy equipment on some nearby construction site. It all comes together just fine. Nobody knows why, only that its regulars are content to leave things at that.

Cooper and I discovered this place when we were eighteen, both of us in our first years at NYU. Of course, discovering it wasn't the same as drinking at it —we were three years under the legal age—but Coop knew somebody who knew somebody, and so did I. We both put out for phony IDs—except the bartenders at The Attic were smart enough to see right through our pathetic subterfuge. We tried to get in at least a dozen times and finally one night the bartender who'd pointed to the door most often told us to give it up, come back when we hit the magic number and he'd buy us each a round.

So we did.

See, our birthdays are only a month apart and remember what I told you before? We've been friends damn near forever. Anyway, The Attic has remained one of our favorite places, especially when you need to feel, you know, relaxed. The music that blasts from the speakers is good, there's always an interesting choice of beers and ale, and maybe best of all it's not a pickup place.

A pickup place is the last kind of place I need this evening.

An old-timer named Charlie is behind the bar. He sees me as I come in and we nod at each other. He raises his eyebrows and jerks his chin at a couple of empty stools at the bar. I shake my head, point at a booth in the corner. I raise two fingers. Charlie nods again and a couple of minutes after I slide into the booth, one of the barmaids puts two large mugs of whatever Charlie has decided is the best beer of the night on the table.

I say thanks.

A second later, Coop sits down across from me. He reaches for one of the mugs, raises it to his mouth and takes a long pull.

"So," he says, "what's the emergency?"

I look at him. "I never said there was an emergency."

"You didn't have to."

He takes another swig of beer. I lift my mug and do the same.

"Sorry to have dragged you away from...whatever."

Coop grins. "I was in the middle of an experiment."

I grin back. "Yeah?"

"Yeah. I'd explain it, but it's probably over your head."

I nod. "Would I be right if I thought if had to do with DNA transfer?"

He laughs. Then his expression turns serious. "So, dude, what's doin'? You sounded like something important was going down."

I avoid the obvious joke. I mean, a couple of minutes of back-and-forth was great, but there's no getting away from my situation.

I take a deep breath. Let it out. Take another...

"Jeez," Coop says, "what in hell happened? One of

those houses of yours fall down a mountainside or something?"

I don't take him up on the chance to do our standard routine, which is him asking me why anyone would pay big bucks for a house built, as he puts it, in the middle of Nature's Nowhere when Manhattan is out there, just waiting. It's light comic relief and we both know it, but light comic relief isn't going to do it for me tonight.

Another breath. In. Out. Then I lean forward. "You remember Bailey?"

"Bailey who?"

"Bailey Abrams. My PA."

"Oh. Sure. Nice girl. Plain-looking, but smart as shit." His brow furrows. "Don't tell me something happened to her."

"No. No, she's fine."

"Well, that's good. I mean, like I said, she's nice. Plus, you'd be out of business without her."

"What?"

"Hey, the lady runs your office. We both know that."

I sigh. Drink some more beer. Look around, catch the barmaid's eye and signal for refills.

"You're right. She does. I'd be lost without her. She's smart and dedicated and efficient and—"

"And she's thinking of quitting?"

"No."

"She wants a big raise and you're asking for my advice?"

"If she asked for a big raise I'd give it to her. And

why would I ask for your advice? I'm the guy with the degree in finance, remember?"

"You're right. If I knew anything about money I'd never have loaned you five bucks for gas our junior year in high school without first getting you to sign an I.O.U."

"Dammit, will you stop fucking around? I have a problem here and—"

The beers arrive. Coop looks at me through narrowed eyes. Then he looks at the barmaid.

"Two burgers," he tells her. "Cheese. Pickles. Onions. Fries." She walks away and he gives me another look. "I have the feeling we're gonna need sustenance to get through whatever comes next. Am I right?"

I hesitate. Then I shrug my shoulders.

"So," Coop says, "what's the deal here?"

I tell him I'm not sure where to start. Coop, ever the rational scientist, suggests that I begin at the beginning.

And I do.

He listens intently as I describe Bailey seeming upset and then losing her cool during a phone conversation with her mother. That impresses him, same as it did me. He knows her for a long time, well enough to find it difficult to imagine her going all emotional.

I explain what the phone call was about. The wedding Saturday in upstate New York. The big family gathering. The pressure from her mom. The pressure from her cousin. The cousin as a lifelong pain in the ass.

The burgers arrive.

We bite into them. They're good—the place has always had great bar food—but my story holds Cooper's attention. I can see him hating Violet and sharing my distress at Bailey's unhappiness.

Then I pause.

"So," I finally say, "I came up with a solution."

Coop chomps down on a french fry. "Damn right, you did." Another chomp. "You offered to play the part of boyfriend and go to the wedding with her."

My jaw would drop, but that wouldn't go over too well considering that I have a mouthful of hamburger.

"How'd you know?"

Coop gives me a pitying look. "How'd I know? I know because, all indications to the contrary, buried deep within that frosty exterior you have a kind heart."

"I do not have a frosty exterior."

"Okay. Maybe not." He wipes his mouth with a napkin. "I know because it's exactly what I would have done in your shoes."

I am amazed how relieved his words make me feel. "Yeah?"

"I mean, what the fuck, it's only one day. Drive up, drive back, put in ten, twelve hours being there for your PA who's been there for you for years —What?"

"It's not one day. It's Friday evening through Sunday morning."

"Oh. Well, that's still doable. I mean, all you give up is one weekend. And you'll be doing a good thing. You gonna eat those fries?"

I wave away the fries. My appetite's gone, maybe because I still haven't told Coop all of it.

"The thing is, it's turning out to be a little more complicated than I'd figured."

"How?"

"Well, for one thing, Bailey pointed out that we'd be under family scrutiny. That she knew a lot about me, but I didn't know a lot about her." I pause. "See, I'm not supposed to be just her date. I'm supposed to be, ah, to be, you know, the dude she's seeing."

"The dude who's fucking her."

I can feel my jaw tighten. "That she's involved with. Yeah."

Coop swipes a fry through a mound of ketchup. "So, what's the problem? The two of you have a couple of conversations—what she likes to do on weekends, favorite music, movie, all that shit—and you're fine."

"We did that. Talked about that stuff, I mean."

"And?"

"And, we talked at her place. So we could get comfortable with each other."

"Great idea."

"Yeah." I pause. "Then I realized it wasn't enough."

"What do you mean, it wasn't enough?"

"Well, being in her apartment is one thing. Being around other people...Different."

"You took her out?"

"Yes. For dinner."

He nods. "How'd that go?"

"Fine." Our eyes meet. I look down and busy myself making wet circles on the wooden table top with my beer mug. I think of that kiss. In the doorway between my kitchen and my garage. And I clear my throat. "It went really well."

"Uh huh."

Is there a question in that 'uh huh'? If there is, I decide to ignore it. For the time being, anyway.

"Then I realized she needed things."

"Things?"

"Clothes. For the weekend. Did you ever notice what she wears?"

"Nope. Not really."

"Yeah, well, that's the point. She doesn't wear anything anybody would notice. Nothing that, you know, makes you realize that she's..."

"A girl?"

"A woman."

"Got it." He grins. "You're really into this thing, dude. I'm proud of you."

"Yeah. Thanks."

"Hey, why so glum? So you're gonna buy her some new clothes and it'll turn out that she's attractive. Right?"

"I already bough the clothes. And she isn't attractive, she's beautiful."

And Cooper, my buddy, my pal, my man-of-science, my beacon-of-truth looks across the table at me, his grin gone, and says, "Shit."

There's no answer to that. I take a pull on my beer instead.

"Have you fucked her?"

It's a simple question, simply stated. I've certainly

thought about fucking Bailey. Hell, it's pretty much all I've thought about. So how come Cooper asking the question, phrasing it with the F-word, makes me bristle? Because, goddammit, I am definitely bristling, and if I was never positive what bristling meant before, I sure as hell know now.

Forget the tight jaw of a few minutes ago. Now, every muscle in my body knots. Worse, the desire to grab Coop by his *My Nobel Prize is Waiting* T-shirt and drag him across the table is so powerful I have to clench my fists to keep from doing it.

"Answer the question, dude. Have you nailed her?"

"No. And stop asking."

"But you want to."

I glare at him. Slap my hands on the table and start to rise to my feet.

"This was a mistake," I say. "I don't even know why we're having this discussion."

"We're having it because you are messed up. Because you need advice. Because you are a man standing on the edge of a cliff. Okay?"

"Listen, Holloway..." I snap my mouth shut and fall back into the seat. "Okay," I mutter. "I am messed up. And, goddammit, I don't even know how it happened."

Coop shrugs. "*My Fair Lady.*"

"What?"

"The play. Or maybe it was a musical. Guy sees girl, sees possibilities, sees a challenge. A makeover, start to finish."

"No. This had nothing to do with possibilities or challenges or makeovers. Well, yes to the makeover part—but only because I wanted to help." I sit back and shake my head. "How was I supposed to know the woman hidden inside Bailey would turn out to be so—so—"

"Fuckable." Coop leans in. "And do not, *do not* tell me that isn't what this is all about, because we both know that it is. You want to take her to bed and screw her brains out, and you know that's out of the question."

"Of course it's out of the question." I look at him. "It *is* out of the question, isn't it?"

"Damn right." Coop checks the room, catches the barmaid's eye and signals for two more beers. "First rule of the road. You don't get involved with women who work for you. It ruins the dynamic. One minute, you're the dude giving orders. The next, you're the dude giving orgasms. No way that can work out, especially once you break up. And, trust me, my man, you will break up."

That, at least, I can agree with. "I know that. I mean, I'm not talking about forever here. I'm just talking about—"

"About fucking. Say the word. Don't give it some deep, sacred meaning just because you're thinking about doing it with a babe you already know as a person."

I smile, and it feels good. "Did you ever consider giving up biomed, or whatever it is you do in that mad scientist's lab of yours, so you could go into psych instead?"

"Hey, did we not spend three weeks in Nepal

together? Okay, it was a dozen years ago, but I remember that stuff. Mindfulness. Joyfulness. What it means. How to see the truth within yourself."

"And?"

"And, look at *your* truth, man. Do you generally know the women you sleep with as persons?"

"Yes. Of course I do. Jesus, Coop, you make me sound like some creep who travels from bed to bed."

"Dude," Coop says in the patient tones of a father explaining the birds and bees to his seven-year-old son, "of course you know things about them. But nothing in depth. It's all sex. It's strictly fun." He pauses. "And here's just a wild guess. Bailey doesn't fit into that 'it's strictly fun' category. Right?"

I sigh. Everything I know about Bailey assures me that he's not just right, he's one hundred percent right.

"On top of which," he adds, "as we have already established, she's not just your employee, she's the one who keeps the wheels from falling off so you can spend your time building houses in the trees."

"I do not build—"

"Bottom line, O'Malley. You'll get her into your bed. You'll have fun. She'll attach a lot more to it than you will. You'll hurt her as a woman, and lose her as an assistant. Still sound good?"

No. It sounds like crap. He's right, and I know it.

The barmaid brings our beers, takes away what's left of our burgers and replaces them with a bowl of popcorn. Yeah, the popcorn should have arrived long before the burgers, but that's one of the things about The Attic. The place doesn't have hard and fast rules, which is good because you need to escape the rules once in while, especially when life is so goddamn full of them.

Like the rule about not sleeping with a woman who works for you. Or the one about not sleeping with a woman who's never in her life had a relationship with a man and is absolutely sure to put more meaning on the act of sex than you will.

"Shit," I say.

Coop flashes me a smug look. "Anybody ever tell you you have a way with words?"

I nod. Then I look at him.

"Thanks," I say.

"Glad to be of help."

"Yeah. I owe you."

"Yup. You do. And you'll still be on the hook even though I'm gonna let you pay for this meal."

He smiles. I smile. I look at the check, take out my wallet, put a couple of twenties on the table and add an outrageously large tip.

Coop and I head out of the bar. Night has fallen. The weather is cool and crisp, and that's the same way I feel. Cool, crisp, and in control.

We pause on the sidewalk.

"Dude," I start to say, "seriously—"

Coop grabs me in a bear hug. I return it.

"Brothers forever," he says gruffly.

"Forever," I repeat.

Because that's how we feel about each other, and I cannot imagine using that particular F-word any other way.

12

And now it's tomorrow.

The day dawns gray and cool. Typical early fall weather or a hint of things to come? I'm not into superstition so I tell myself it can't be the latter as I pull up in front of Bailey's apartment building, but I have to admit I'm, well, not nervous. Not exactly. Wary, is a better way to describe it.

No way I'm going to let Bailey know it.

It's twelve noon on the nose, and she is waiting for me at the curb. She's wearing her new jeans, the new white T and the white—what are they called? Mules. The apricot jacket is slung over her arm. The outfit is casual and she looks...spectacular, is the only word that works.

She's even left her hair loose.

Yes. She looks spectacular indeed. Good enough to eat...and that isn't a phrase that should be in my head.

She also looks terrified. Uh oh. Not terrified. Grim.

Determined. It doesn't take a genius to figure out what's happened.

Well, fuck. We're going to have to change that.

I smile as I get out of the 'Vette. "Hi."

"Hi," she says. No answering smile.

I reach for her suitcase. So does she. We both grab the handle and fight for possession. Enough.

"Bailey?"

"Yes?"

"Let go."

"Mr. O'Malley. I've been thinking..."

I let go of the handle, straighten up, fold my arms over my chest and give her what I hope is a stern look.

"What did you call me?"

She swallows hard. "Matthew. What I mean is..."

"What you mean is, you've thought things over and this isn't going to work."

She heaves a sigh of relief. "Exactly."

"Because you won't be able to pull it off. Or I won't be able to pull it off. Or Verifiably Vile Vi is so smart she'll see right through us."

"She knows me. Everybody in my family knows me. And—"

"They think they know you, but I'm the man who actually does. I know the true Bailey. The one who's been just standing by and waiting to greet the world all these years."

She sighs. "If only that were true."

"It *is* true."

"Have you forgotten the old saying? Clothes don't make the man. Well, the woman. I'm still me inside."

"Yes. You are. And that's a damn good thing, because you are and always have been a smart, strong, proud, brave, altogether remarkable woman. The only change is that you're no longer hiding any of who you are from the world."

"That's a fine pep talk. But—"

"It's the truth. You're all those things." I put my hand under her chin and gently urge her to lift her face and meet my gaze. "You're also beautiful."

"It's the clothes."

"I thought we just agreed that clothes don't make the woman. Trust me. You are beautiful."

Her eyes glitter. Her lips curve in a smile. "I'd settle for pretty."

"Never settle," I say and then, only because it's the right thing to do, I lower my head and kiss her mouth, and hell, even if it's the wrong thing to do, I'm happy I did it.

I HAVE a GPS but my ever-efficient PA has Googled directions and printed them out. It's a great plan. I'd rather listen to Bailey than the robotic voice of my GPS.

We make surprisingly good time once we get out of Manhattan and across the George Washington Bridge. We take the Palisades Parkway for a few miles. I know it from a couple of ski trips. It's a handsome road that cuts through the trees.. Bailey, it turns out, has never gone this way before. She always takes the train when she goes home to visit.

"If I'd known how nice this road is," she says, "I'd have driven. Maybe that's what I'll do next time."

"Or we could drive it for a while some Sunday. There are lots of little towns just off this parkway. I bet they have some pretty nice restaurants."

I hear myself say this as if planning a future weekend together is a natural thing to do. I tell myself I'm simply getting into the role I'm about to play, but when I glance over at Bailey, she's doing that teeth-sinking-into-her-tender-bottom-lip routine.

My gut clenches.

The hell it does. Just that fast, what clenches is my dick, except dicks don't clench. What they do is get hard. And harder...

I shift my weight.

I look at Bailey again. She's looking at me and there's a sudden sweep of pink in her face. Has she noticed the little tent that's formed in my lap?

"So," she says brightly, "did you ever wonder about that?"

Crap! "Look, I apologize. I mean, it isn't deliberate—"

"Why they call some roads parkways and others highways? Or expressways. Like the Long Island Expressway. And then in California they're freeways. Isn't that right? Whenever I read a book set there, like those Elvis Cole novels by, what's his name, Robert Crais, he's always talking about freeways..."

She's babbling, but I am grateful for the change in subject. Not only is it a diversion, it's interesting. Turns out we both like the same authors and when one word leads to another, I end up admitting I tried reading *War and Peace* back in college and never managed to finish it.

"It just seemed dead to me," I tell her, and she assures me it was that way for her too until she reached this one particular chapter, and—

And, I'm getting to know more and more about my pretend-girlfriend.

And, dammit, I like what I'm getting to know.

So much so that after a while, in the middle of an exchange about which is the better band, the ancient The Who or the equally ancient Rolling Stones, I reach for her hand, thread my fingers through hers and we clasp the gear shifter together.

Wrong move, the voice in my head says.

The voice is Coop's, and I ignore it just as I ignore it when we stop for coffee and I put my arm around Bailey's waist as we walk back to the car.

I even drop a kiss on her temple.

Big mistake, Coop says.

I know he's right. There won't be any kissing. Not on this trip. Not unless we have to do some convincing for Vainglorious Violet—and this is the first time I have ever even thought that word, vainglorious, in my entire life.

The kissing-touching thing is just practice.

The voice in my head snickers, I tell it to do us both a favor and shut the fuck up.

And, after a while, it does.

WE DON'T SEEM to run out of things to talk about.

We even talk football.

"It isn't only whatever you called it," I tell Bailey. "A bunch of guys beating each other into the dirt. Sure, it's physical, but it's also mental. A lot mental."

She makes a scoffing sound.

I shake my head.

I explain a few simple plays. I describe the decisions a quarterback faces when he sees the defense lining up, the decisions the defense has to make in those same seconds.

She admits that maybe she's misjudged the game and I tell her she has and when we watch a game together, she'll see that it's more like a chess game than she thought.

She laughs. "Uh huh. Except with four hundred pound chessmen," she says.

I grin. "Three hundred pounds," I say, "but who's counting?"

The time passes quickly and before long, we reach Schenectady. It turns out to be something halfway between a city and a town, at least that's how it strikes me. It's old, some of it is handsome, some is tired looking, and some is emerging into twenty-first century life. I like what I see, but it turns out Bailey actually grew up just outside Schenectady in a place called Washingtonville.

She asks if I want a quick tour. I tell her that would be great—and it is. Seeing the turf that was once hers is kind of like seeing her when she was a kid.

The house she grew up in is a comfortable-looking white colonial with black shutters and a deep porch. There's an old rocker just visible at one end; Bailey says she used to sit there for hours, her nose buried in a book, and I can tell she's glad to see the chair is still there.

The elementary and middle schools are a couple of miles away; past them is the high school. We drive by the library—she also spent lots of time there, she says with a wistful smile. Then we head up Main Street and yeah, that's really its name. Same as in far too many small American towns, there are several shuttered stores, but there are also signs of renewed economic life: a Thai restaurant, a crafts shop, what looks like a small art gallery. We agree that's all good to see.

The inn is just outside the town. On the way, we pass a structure that looks like a badly decorated birthday cake.

It's the country club, Bailey says. The scene of tomorrow's spectacular.

The Wedding.

"You'll hate it," she assures me. "I mean, you cannot imagine how awful it will be."

I shift gears as we start up a steep hill.

"Did I ever tell you about the O'Malley family get-togethers?"

She looks at me. "No. And believe me, Matthew, whatever you're going to say—".

"*Matthew O'Malley,*'" I say in my best Uncle Harry

voice, *"how old are you now? Ten? My, you've grown so big! Not as tall as your cousin David, of course, but at least you're not a midget anymore. Too bad David couldn't be here, but he's at MIT on a teen science retreat."*

Bailey smiles. "Okay, So we all have horrible memories of weddings and family parties when we were kids, but—"

"Hello there, young man. Remember me? We haven't seen each other in years. Your cousin David said to send you his best. He can't be here. He's at Oxford, starting his Fulbright scholarship. And what's new with you, Matt. Anything?"

I get a giggle this time. "All right. Family gatherings can be tough, but—"

"It's Matt, right? Haven't seen you in—must be a decade. David sends his regards. Couldn't get here. He's giving a speech at TED tomorrow. TED. You know, that incredibly prestigious organization? He's talking about sperm donations. Specifically his. He's so brilliant that Cambridge is setting up a chair in his name. Well, actually, not a chair. A giant sperm bank. They want a thousand women with genius level IQs to bear his babies."

Bailey roars with laughter. "You're making that up."

I grin. "Yeah, but it's close enough to the truth. I hate these big family things. They're like giant contests that are fun for everybody but the contestants."

Bailey's laugh turns into a sigh. "Violet loves them."

"Violet's in for a fall. Bride or not, you'll be the star of the show."

"Me in disguise, you mean."

"The real you. No disguise. You were always who you are, honey. You just hid the truth from the world."

Bailey gets a serious look on her face. "Matthew. I don't know how to thank you. For everything. For all you've done—for all you're doing. I can never repay you. For the clothes, yes. But for all the rest..."

"Hey." I smile at her as we crest the hill. "Who knows? You might have to do the same for me some day. Nobody can ever predict when these little family dramas are going to rear their ugly heads."

She laughs. So do I.

Little do I know the dangerous truth of what I thought was just a throwaway line.

AT FIRST GLANCE, the inn is not my kind of place.

I am, as you know, into structural simplicity. Clean lines. High ceilings. Lots of wood, glass and light.

The inn is pure Victoriana. Turrets. Gables. Asymmetrical porches. It's gingerbread at its worst...Until you take a second look and realize that maybe it's gingerbread at its best.

Somebody built this place in the late eighteenth century and somebody in the twenty-first is taking very good care of it. It's an antique, after all, and if you have any feeling for history, you've got to admire its out-of-date beauty.

Our suite—and Bailey's right, it's really just one big room—is on the third floor with a nice view of what turns out to be a leafy bend in the Mohawk River. We even have a little balcony overlooking the water. The room itself is handsome. Is it the inn's idea of a bridal suite? A presidential suite? It doesn't matter because it is, as I say, handsome, which is a nice bonus. The walls are covered in what seems to be pale yellow silk; there's some kind of Oriental carpet underfoot; the furniture is big, suitable for the room's dimensions. The expected sofa bed is big as well, and I'm sure I won't have any problem fitting my six feet three inch self into it...

But it's going to be a lot to ask when the real bed, all the way at the opposite end of the room, is so spectacular.

For openers, it's enormous. Did the Victorians go in for king-size beds? I don't care; I only know that this thing is huge. And it's handsome. The mahogany headboard is a masterpiece of carved leaves and unicorns. The comforter is white and lush. Gold pillows dot the snowy landscape.

And it has a canopy hung with gold silk.

My PA makes a little oooh sound. I don't blame her. It's the kind of bed that deserves an oooh. It deserves even more—and, dammit, I am not going to think about that.

I turn away, drop our luggage next to a bureau that's at least half a mile long, and make the pilgrimage to the bathroom. I definitely don't want to see Victorian plumbing fixtures...

And, man, I don't.

The bathroom is almost the size of Bailey's apartment. It's a sea of white. White marble floor and walls.

White fixtures, including an enormous soaking tub. But don't get me wrong. There's also glass. Plenty of it. As in a standalone glass shower stall with multiple spray heads and a teak bench so that the ten or twenty people showering in the stall could sit down and take a break while they waited for the other team to come onto the field.

Or so that one man and one woman could make love with all those sprays going and then try something a little slower, a little more inventive, on that bench...

"It's time," Bailey says from behind me.

I turn and look at her.

"Time for what?" I say, a little hoarsely.

"The rehearsal dinner. It's at seven, remember?"

I can hardly remember my own name, but I nod and mumble Yes, right, and I tell Bailey I'll just check out the coffee machine the desk clerk—and yes, he's the guy she knew in high school although at first, he didn't recognize her and when he did, I could damn near see his wisdom teeth when his mouth dropped open.

Forget that. I tell her I'll get coffee while she gets ready, and then I make my exit.

THE DINNER IS at a restaurant in Troy, which turns out to be a smallish city just a few miles away.

My PA looks fantastic.

The blue silk dress. The butterfly shoes we bought at Saks. Her hair is loose. She has on a black silk jacket and I'm almost sorry to see it because it means I won't have any reason to take off my own jacket and wrap her in it later tonight, when we're on our way back to our room, and for some crazy reason the thought of me taking something off and her putting it on is a turn-on.

Hell.

She's quiet during our drive to the restaurant. I figure that she's nervous, but when I glance over at her, her expression is calm.

"Hey," I say.

She looks at me.

"You okay?" I ask.

She nods.

"Have I told you how fantastic you look?"

She nods again.

"Because you do. Look fantastic—"

"I'm okay," she says quietly. "Stop worrying about me."

"I'm not worrying. I just want you to have a good time tonight. This shouldn't only be about your cousin. It should be about you. Understand?"

I pull up in front of the restaurant. The place is lit up like Times Square on New Year's Eve. Two kids in white jackets that make them look like ice cream salesmen trot towards us. One aims for my side of the car, the other for Bailey's.

"Tonight isn't really about Violet or me," she says softly. "It's about you, Matthew, and what a wonderful man you are."

She leans over and presses her lips lightly to my cheek, and I swear, I can feel everything inside me melting. I want to take her in my arms. Hold her. Kiss her...

Good Humor Boy number one yanks the door open.

"Your keys, sir?" he says, his eyes shining at the prospect of getting his hands on my 'Vette.

I swallow hard, get out of the car and hand the boy the keys and a bill. His eyes get even shinier.

"Park somewhere safe," I tell him. "No scratches when I get my car back and you'll get a second fifty. And if I even suspect you went for a joy ride, you'll be attending high school in Antarctica next semester. Got that?"

Bailey laughs as I walk around the car to her. She loops her arm through mine.

"So much for Mister Wonderful," I say, because it's safer than what I want to say, even if I'm not quite sure what that is.

She smiles up at me and before she can answer, a middle-aged woman shrieks. And gallops towards us.

"BAILEY!"

My PA takes a deep breath. "Showtime," she whispers, and we're off and running.

THE SHRIEKER IS Bailey's mother.

She also turns out to be a nice woman, once we get past the necessary maternal preliminaries.

"Why didn't you stop by my condo? Why didn't you call and let me know you were here? I was worried.

After all, who knows how many car crashes happen each day? What did you do to yourself? Did you get a haircut? You look—different." When she finally pauses for breath, she turns her attention to me. "Aren't you going to introduce me to your young man?"

"Mom. This is Mr. O'Malley, my—"

I stick out my hand. "Hello, Mrs. Abrams. I'm Matt O'Malley. Bailey's told me a lot about you."

Mom tilts her head to the side. She's doing an appraisal, and I fight the urge to straighten my tie.

"Mr. O'Malley," she says.

"Please. Call me Matt."

"My daughter works for you, right?"

"She does."

"And now long have you and she been—involved? Because I'm surprised she never mentioned it until a few days ago."

There it is. A direct shot across the bow.

"Three months," I say.

"Three weeks," says Bailey.

I laugh. Or I say *ha ha* and hope it sounds like a laugh. "Time's flown, hasn't it, sweetheart?"

"Flown," Bailey says, and adds her own version of a laugh.

Mrs. Abrams looks from one of us to the other. There's no way to read what she's thinking, but just when I start figuring we have flunked the first test, she smiles, steps up and takes my free arm.

"If I had a man who looks like you, Mr. O'Malley, I'd keep you a secret as long as possible. Why ask for competition?"

"It's Matt. And there is no competition, Mrs. Abrams. How could there be, when your daughter is in my life?"

Bailey's mom giggles. "It's Rose," she says, "and I can hardly wait to introduce you to the family."

We head into the crowd.

It's pretty clear people are surprised to see Bailey, or to see her looking like this, or maybe to see her with an attentive date. That's the role I'm playing and believe me, it isn't difficult. The truth is, I'm enjoying this. It's kind of like me being the only person who knew there was a butterfly tucked inside a plain brown paper wrapper, and now everybody else knows it too. Okay, it's a mixed metaphor, but you get my meaning.

Besides, people are greeting my PA with genuine warmth.

It's good to see.

Bailey is dealing with it well, but she's still nervous. I can tell because I'm holding her hand and it's icy cold, plus she's shaking. Not enough so you'd notice, but I can feel the tiny tremors going through her.

"You're doing fine," I whisper, leaning down and putting my mouth to her ear.

Bad move.

I end up inhaling her fragrance. Yes, lemon. What did she call it? Lemon verbena. Maybe. Or maybe it's just Bailey. Whatever it is, I like the scent. I want to bury my nose in her hair and take the smell of her deep into my lungs.

I break stride only long enough to grab a flute of champagne from a tray and down it in one gulp. She does the same and quickly exchanges the empty flute for a full one.

"Easy," I whisper.

She looks up at me. "Chester doesn't approve of alcohol. This stuff is probably colored club soda. I just need something to do with my hands."

Even here, with what looks like a million people around us, I have no difficulty thinking of other things she could do with her hands.

"Come on, you two," Mama Rose says.

We could. Come. I certainly could, and I am sure I could make my gorgeous PA come right along with me...

Another tray-bearing server is slipping through the crowd. I grab a glass—red wine, this time, unless its Kool Aid—and drink half of it. Bailey does the same.

"Mr. O'Malley," Mama Rose says. She gives a girlish giggle. "I mean, Matt. Say hello to Bailey's Aunt Martha."

I say hello to Aunt Martha. And to cousin Janet. Cousin Billy. Uncle Saul. Uncle Jeffrey. A pair of twins. A trio of triplets. And that's just the beginning. Mama Rose is already tugging us towards the next batch of relatives.

All of them do subtle double takes when they see Bailey. I don't blame them. She's left beautiful behind. Now, she's spectacular. It isn't only the way she looks. It's also the way she's handling herself. I can see the tension going out of her. She's turning into the Bailey nobody but I seem to have known: funny, smart, at ease with the world.

The real woman has come out of hiding, and she's getting stronger by the minute.

As for the relatives—after a while, I give up trying to remember names. There are so many people at this rehearsal dinner that it's hard to imagine any of tomorrow night's wedding guests have been left out.

Some have, but I won't know that until tomorrow night.

As for the bride and groom—they have not yet put in an appearance, but the bride's parents are front and center.

When I am introduced to them, Violet's mother tells me that Elevator Boy—she refers to him as *our darling Chester*—paid for all the festivities.

"He owns a cleaning business," she says proudly.

"A launderette," my PA says, so sweetly that I wonder if s it's possible to get a sugar high just from hearing those words. She smiles angelically as she snags a glass of something from a server. "You must be so happy for Violet."

Violet's father nods. Violet's mother isn't quite as gullible. Her eyes narrow to slits.

"*Three* launderettes," she says.

"Oh, of course. Silly me. Chester owns *three* launderettes," Bailey says, looking up at me with an expression of total innocence. "You know what a launderette is, don't you, Matthew? It's one of those places where you feed coins into a slot and then you get to wash your sheets in the same machine where somebody else just washed poopy diapers. Such an amazing invention!"

I almost choke on a mouthful of the red swill I'm drinking.

"Are you all right, sweetheart?" my PA-turned-Vixen says.

Sweetheart? I nod and pat my lips with a paper napkin embossed with the names of the happy couple held in the beak of a golden dove.

I could swear the bird winks at me.

"I'm fine," I say.

Bailey smiles. "Good. Because the night is young."

Man. If this is just the start of the evening, what comes next? Is Bailey drinking too much? I doubt it. Sure, she's had three drinks in maybe fifteen minutes, but she's right about the bubbly stuff tasting nothing like champagne. The red stuff is definitely wine, but still, it's only wine.

"Where *is* Violet?" my PA asks. "I can hardly wait to congratulate her."

Violet's mother doesn't answer the question. She's suddenly staring at Bailey as if she's never seen her before.

"My goodness," she says slowly, "whatever have you done to yourself, Bailey? You look—you look—"

"Magnificent!"

This, from Violet's father. It's the first word he's uttered and from the look his wife shoots him and the way he shrinks into his suit, I figure it might be his last for the night.

"Different," she says coldly. She turns her attention back to Bailey. "New clothes? New hairstyle? Makeup? I can't quite put my finger on it."

I have been holding my drink in one hand and Bailey's hand in the other. Now, my PA kind of turns towards me so that her body is pressed to mine. She rests her fingers lightly on my chest. Instinctively, I let go of her elbow and slide my arm around her waist.

"Mostly, what's different is having Matthew in my life," she purrs.

She turns that lovely face up to mine and after maybe a tenth of a second hesitation, I bend down and kiss her. It's as natural as it was to put my arm around her and it's only a light kiss, just the brush of my mouth over hers.

Why not? It's part of the game.

But when I look into her eyes, I know three things.

One. Bailey is not the slightest bit drunk. She is simply enjoying her coming-out party.

Two. The game has taken on new dimensions.

Three. To hell with Bailey being my PA.

Tonight, she is my woman.

13

Mama Rose goes off in a different direction.

Bailey and I keep circulating until we've said hello to, I am certain, every human being in the county.

When Bailey starts to exchange her now-empty glass for a full one, I stop her.

"You don't need it," I say quietly. "You're doing just fine on your own."

She nods. "I hope so," she whispers.

I bring her hand to my lips. Lots of eyes are on us. People are talking about us; I'm a guy so I'm not usually good at knowing these things, but even I can tell we're the object of lots of speculation. So, yeah, we're being watched, but that isn't why I'm kissing Bailey's hand.

I'm doing it because she's Bailey, and Violet's father got it right.

She's magnificent.

She always has been. I always knew that, only not

the way I know it now. What I mean is, I saw her as intelligent and dedicated and creative and generous. Now I see her as all those things and more. And it isn't because my duckling has turned into a swan. I told you right away, I'm the kind of dude who's always done just fine with women, so having a beautiful woman on my arm is nothing new.

Yes, but this beautiful woman is Bailey. At the risk of sounding corny, she's beautiful inside as well as out.

"You're amazing," I tell her. "And I'm proud to be your lover."

She blushes. I'm not her lover; we both know that. But there's a feeling between us, a link…

A tension.

Jesus.

I want to sweep her into my arms and carry her out of this place, to our room at the inn.

"Bailey," I say with whispered urgency, "Bailey…"

She stiffens. And says, "They're here!"

And so they are. Cousin Violet and Elevator Boy have just come through the door.

No surprises about either of them.

Bailey's description of Chester was dead accurate. He's short and paunchy. Yes, he almost surely wears shoes with lifts to give him added height. Not that they do much good. No matter how you look at him, he's small, and he walks with that sort of aggressively Napoleonic strut some small men seem to need to get through life. What Bailey left out was that he combs his hair sideways from one ear to the other, but the strands are few and far between so the style, if you want to call it that, doesn't do much to cover his shiny scalp. He's wearing a dark suit and shiny black shoes. Thanks to Bailey's description, I pretty much see him wearing those shoes with Bermudas. I also see him as shirtless, and I try hard not to dwell on that.

Violet is...Let's just say there's not a guy out there who hasn't seen his fill of Violets. Lots of hair in a color not produced by nature, every strand shellacked into place. Lots of makeup. A dress that's too short, too tight, too sparkly, too everything unless the woman wearing it carries a baton and is followed by seventy six trombones—and yes, my Mom loves that old movie so as a kid, I probably saw it a million times.

Even from here, I can see the diamond glinting on her finger.

It looks less like a diamond than a headlight.

Subtlety is definitely not Vi's middle name.

I tend to be a doodler. I guess it goes with designing things. If I were doodling Violet, she'd be a bunch of circles. Maybe some dudes are into that. The overly curved thing. Not me. The architect in me prefers the elegance of linear structures.

Like my Bailey.

There's a grand piano in the corner. A guy's been noodling at it, and now he bangs out a few chords and leans into a mike that's on top of the piano.

"Ladies and gentlemen, the bride and groom!"

There's applause. A couple of cheers. Violet clings to her groom's arm. Maybe she's afraid he'll turn and run. She waves. Marie Antoinette couldn't do it better. More cheers. She and Elevator Boy move forward.

Violet looks around the room at the peasants. She is beaming. Her gaze skims over the aunts, the uncles, the cousins, the parents, us...

Her gaze sweeps back.

And settles on Bailey.

I can almost hear what she's thinking. *Who is that woman? Could it be...No. It isn't. Wait. It is. No. It isn't...*

Chester is trying to head for his parents, but Violet has other ideas. She tugs one way. He tugs the other. They tussle silently for a couple of seconds, but she wins the war.

They're coming straight through the crowd. To us.

"Matthew," my PA, my Bailey, whispers. "Maybe this wasn't such a good idea after all."

I still have my arm around her. And I can feel her starting to tremble.

"Baby," I say, just loud enough so the people nearest to us can hear me.

She looks up at me. And, no hesitation this time, I lower my head and claim her mouth. It's trembling too, and I kiss her until her lips soften and, crowd or no crowd, she gives herself up to me.

It isn't easy to end the kiss, but I do.

Vituperative Vi and Napoleon the Launderette Tycoon are standing before us.

"Bailey?" Violet says.

She sounds the way I figure Stanley must have sounded when he confronted Dr. Livingston.

I keep my arm around my woman. "Violet," she says, and I want to cheer because her tone is firm and calm.

"Aunt Rose said you were coming, but I didn't actually believe..."

"Hi," I say briskly. I stick out my hand. Napoleon takes it. It's like holding onto a dead fish and when I let go, I fight back the desire to wipe my fingers against my trousers. "I'm Matt O'Malley." I turn to Violet and hold out my hand again. She takes it and I know that the happy couple has at least the dead fish thing in common. "It's my fault Bailey didn't get back to you sooner." I draw my girl closer to my side. "I have to admit, I didn't want us to give up our long weekend in the Hamptons. We don't get the chance to get out there as often as we'd like."

Okay. I'm lying. But not completely. I do like the Hamptons. Bailey likes Jones Beach. Sure, one's pricey real estate and one's a public park, but so what? They're both out east on Long Island, and ol' Vi isn't likely to know the difference.

Yeah, but she hasn't bought into the whole story either. Not quite yet.

"So," she says, looking at Bailey, "this is your boss?"

"Well, yes. Matthew is—"

"I hope I'm much more than that," I say with a quick smile. "Right, honey?"

Bailey looks up at me. The situation is getting to her. I can see it. Actually, I can feel it. Her posture has stiffened.

"And you've been—dating—for how long?"

The *dating* drips with innuendo. I wait a beat. Bailey remains silent. I can't believe she's going to let this round go to Violet.

"Three weeks," I say.

"Three months," Bailey says.

We've both tried to make up for the mistake we made with Vi's parents earlier.

"Time flies," I say softly, and I touch the tip of my index finger to Bailey's lips.

She lets out a little breath. And smiles. Hey, I am nothing if not a problem-solver.

Violet isn't satisfied. Her eyes—they're piggy eyes, kind of small and too close together—narrow. Must be a family trait.

"Which is it?" she demands. "Three weeks? Or three months?"

And just that fast, Bailey takes control.

"Three months," she says. "But we didn't let anyone at the office know until three weeks ago. It wouldn't have been good protocol." She flashes me a sexy glance from under half-lowered lashes. "Then it just got so difficult to keep our hands off each other, even in the office..."

Napoleon's eyebrows try to fly into his non-existent hairline. Violet's mouth drops open. I know a cue when I hear one, and I happily perform what is clearly becoming my night's duty again.

I smile, lower my head, and kiss my woman.

And my woman kisses me back.

THE EVENING GOES QUICKLY.

Violet and Napoleon sail off to conquer the crowd,

although anyone can see it's my girl who's done the conquering. She jokes, she smiles, she talks, she listens. She's finally the woman she's always been—she just kept that woman hidden.

I am enthralled.

I love watching her. Love listening to her, even when she decides to take on Uncle Arthur. Uncle Arthur is my Uncle Harry by a different name. He's got an opinion on everything, and he's convinced his opinions are facts.

People roll their eyes.

Bailey rolls her intellect.

She and Uncle Arthur debate the world scene. The national economy. Climate change. The environment. Bailey is firm but polite. And when Uncle Arthur suddenly grins, grabs both her hands, kisses her on each cheek and says he loves how she stands up to him, it's all I can do not to applaud.

There's a buffet, and we eat. Not much, though. Neither of us seems to have an appetite.

There's also music. Soft, easy stuff. A drummer and a bassist join the pianist and a few couples take over the miniscule dance floor.

I start leading Bailey to it. She holds back.

"I don't dance," she says.

I shrug. "That's good, because neither do I."

It's not really true. I'm not John Travolta, but I can manage. Still, the white lie works. She holds my hand and we head for the dance floor, where she goes into my arms. She's a little stiff, but I stroke my hand down and back and tell her to just feel the music, and after a few minutes, she does.

Good. All I want is to give her family yet another view of this woman they've only discovered tonight...

Come on, O'Malley. Be honest.

What I want is an excuse to hold her in my arms. Like this. Just like this. Her head on my shoulder. Her hair silky and soft against my jaw. My hands at the base of her spine, gently urging her to come closer. And she does. She moves into me. Leans against me. Presses the length of her soft, sweet body against mine.

She sighs and winds her arms around my neck.

I nuzzle a curl away from her ear. I feel her tremble, but I know that this time it isn't from fear.

We've been moving slowly, staying with the soft music. We've reached the edge of the little dance floor. There's a hallway beyond it that probably leads to another room. It's barely lit and I dance us into those waiting shadows.

She gets even closer to me. I feel her hands in the hair at the nape of my neck.

I've managed to control my body. Until now. But the feel of her breasts against me, her thighs...

The inevitable happens.

My erection rises hot and hard against her.

"Hell," I murmur. "Bailey. Honey, I'm sorry..."

She leans back in my arms. You know that thing they say? About a woman's eyes filling with stars? Turns out it isn't just a line. It's true. I can see starlight and moonlight and all the promises a man could ever want glittering in her beautiful eyes.

And she moves against me. Delicately. But deliberately. She moves, and I grit my teeth to keep from lifting her in my arms and carrying her into the waiting shadows.

"Bailey." My voice is low. A warning growl. "Bailey," I say again, and she silences me by rising on her toes and pressing her lips to mine.

Then she clasps my face between her hands.

"Matthew," she whispers. "Please. Take me to bed."

14

W e slip away without saying anything to anyone.

There's a door in that dark hallway and we use it. It leads to the parking lot and, dammit, where's the kid who parked my car?

I am holding Bailey tight against me. My hand is splayed over her hip and I can feel the heat of her skin right through her sexy blue dress.

There he is. The kid in the white jacket who parked my car.

"Hey," I say, and he jumps a little. I don't think he's accustomed to the restaurant patrons appearing at this end of the lot.

"Yessir?"

I fumble in my jacket pocket, find the little plastic card he gave me and hand it over. "The Corvette."

"Yessir. I remember. I parked it way in the back, where it would be safe."

Right now, nothing is safe. Bailey is burrowing against me. I need to get us away from here. Fast.

I hand the kid a fifty. ""Get the car to me in less than two minutes and I'll double that," I say.

He looks from me to Bailey and then to me again.

"Yessir!"

He trots off. Maybe sixty seconds later, the 'Vette roars up to where we're standing. The kid gets out; I fork over the other fifty. He looks at it and gives me a goofy grin.

"Hey, thanks, man..."

We are in the car and gone.

I reach for Bailey's hand. It's cool. Her fingers are shaking. I bring her hand to my mouth and kiss it. Then we clasp the gear shifter together and I step hard on the gas.

It took us twenty minutes to get here.

It takes us ten to get back.

A fast trip...but long enough for a faint glint of sanity to pierce my brain.

In other words, just as we pull up at the inn, Coop's voice is in my head.

Dude! What the fuck are you doing?

I'm supposed to be helping Bailey stand up to her cousin. A masquerade. A no-sex, no involvement, no-nothing-but-me-playing-Good-Samaritan game.

Who am I kidding?

It stopped being that the first time I held my PA in my arms. Sure, I was only trying to comfort her...And I did. I have. The problem is that the more I comforted her, the more I got to know her, the more she became a woman, a very special woman, as opposed to being my assistant.

She whispers my name.

I take a deep breath.

The same saffron-robed monk who taught me the concept of joyfulness taught me the value of mindfulness. How to leave the body and reach for your center.

Breathe in. Hold for a five-count. Breathe out. Slowly. That's it. Repeat. And again...

Bailey makes a little sound. She reaches for the door. "It's okay," she says in a small, shaky voice. "I understand."

No. She does not understand. I know she's thinking I don't want her and, God, she's all I want, all I've truly, honestly, deeply wanted in a very long time. I'm what she wants too, but is this the right thing to do? Will taking Bailey to bed be wrong? Cooper would think it's wrong. My sister would think it's wrong. Yes, but Coop and Casey have nothing to do with this. This is about Bailey and me.

To hell with mindfulness, with logic, with sanity. I'm out of the car and around it so fast that she has no choice but to step into my arms.

"No," she says, "no, Matthew, I underst..."

I kiss her. I cup her face and kiss her, gently at first and then harder and deeper. She responds and when she does, I clasp her hand and bring it between us. I need her to know, positively know, how much I want her.

The desk clerk gave me a key to the front door.

"We lock up at ten," he'd said.

A damn good thing, because if I had to stop to get a key right now I'd probably vault the desk and grab the poor bastard by the throat if he took more than a second to give it to me.

I dredge the key from my pocket and fumble with it —my hands are not as steady as they might be. Then we're inside and somehow we get up the stairs to our room.

The question of whether or not this is a bridal suite has been answered. At the very least it's a suite for romance, and for this night.

The lamps on the bedside tables have been turned on. Turned on low, so that the bed is softly lit. A bottle of champagne is chilling in a bucket beside one of the lamps. The comforter has been turned down and a long stemmed red rose lies on each of our pillows.

A dude with a thing for sarcasm might say all that's missing is soft music, but I am not that dude tonight.

What I am is a man who wants only to make love to his woman.

I elbow the door shut and turn to her.

"Bailey," I say thickly.

She smiles. Then she is in my arms, our mouths fused in a kiss so intense it almost drives me to my knees.

I peel off her black silk jacket.

She pushes my suit coat back on my shoulders. I shrug it off; it falls to the floor. I turn her around, push her hair aside and press my mouth to the nape of her neck. She makes a little sound that sends my already racing pulse into overdrive. It's a sigh, a moan, a primal admission of need that rocks me to my core.

I tell myself to move slowly. Not to lose control. That's not going to be easy. What I want is to pull up her skirt, tear off whatever she's wearing under it, unzip my fly and take her here, right against the wall.

But I don't.

Instead, I draw her further into the room. I tilt up her chin, kiss her mouth, gently turn her around and find the zipper tab at the back of her dress.

Slowly, I begin pulling it down, exposing her lovely shoulders to my eyes.

Her skin is pale gold in the lamplight. It begs to be kissed and I oblige, kissing the nape of her neck, and as I kiss, I bring the zipper lower and lower until the dress lies open to the base of her spine.

Just below the zipper, I see a hint of black.

I touch my finger to it. It's silk. Panties. Black silk panties. I hold her by the hips, bend to her, kiss that sliver of silk.

Bailey moans. Her hands bunch at her sides.

I slip my hand inside the dress.

The silk is as warm and smooth as her skin. I remind myself to go slow, but I can't resist cupping her ass, sliding my hands to her ass, then moving one hand forward forward...

Cupping her.

Ah, God!

She's hot as flame. And wet. She's soaked, and I don't know which of us moans first, she or I. as all that heat and dampness kisses my palm.

I turn her towards me. She's more than beautiful. Her head is thrown back. Her lashes are lowered. Her lips are parted and her cheeks are flushed.

I cup her shoulders.

"Sweetheart," I whisper. "Open your eyes. Look at me."

I want her watching me as I undress her.

As I make love to her.

As I make her mine.

Slowly, her lashes lift.

Even more slowly, I draw the blue silk dress down. When it reaches her breasts, she clasps my wrists.

I kiss her.

She lets go of my wrists. I lower my head and kiss the lovely slope of her breasts.

She is breathing hard. Sighing. Trembling.

I tug at the dress. It slides to her waist. To her hips.

It falls to the floor. I take her hand and she steps free of it.

I groan.

The sight of her is beyond anything I've imagined and now, in a rush of sharp honesty, I know I've been living this in my dreams for a long time, this moment of seeing what was hidden within those baggy suits because some part of me always knew my Bailey was like this.

Lovely. Incredibly lovely.

And look at what she's wearing!

A lacy black bra that makes an offering of her breasts. Panties that are nothing more than a tiny black triangle. And, sweet Jesus, thigh high stockings with those spiked heels...

"Casey," she whispers.

I blink. "My sister?"

"She insisted. She said if I were going to be different, I had to feel different straight down to my skin."

I grin. My sister's some piece of work, but I don't want her in my head right now, especially because I suddenly recall what she'd said about not hurting Bailey. Hurting her is the last thing I want to do, but...

"What?" Bailey asks.

I hesitate. "I just thought..." I hesitate again. "This wasn't supposed to happen."

"This?"

I nod. "You. Me. I don't want to do anything you don't want..."

My shy, quiet, reserved PA digs her hands into my hair and hauls my face down to hers.

"If you knew anything about what I want," she says fiercely, "you'd know that I've wanted this forever. You. Me. Exactly like this."

I swing her into my arms and silence her with a kiss as I carry her to the bed. She reaches for me, but I'm unbuttoning my shirt, toeing off my shoes and socks, undoing my belt...

"Hell!" I shake my head. "I don't have a condom."

Bailey smiles. "It's okay. I'm on the pill."

Good. Great. Two questions answered. Yes, we can fuck. And no, that ridiculous idea I had a while back about her being a virgin is just that. Ridiculous.

I leave on my boxers. Not that they're hiding much.

I am big to begin with. I think I already told you that. Now, I am more than big. My dick feels enormous, and from the way Bailey gasps when she looks at the tent my erection has made in my boxers, enormous may just be the appropriate word.

I sit down next to her.

"I want to see you," I whisper, and I ease her up against the pillows, reach behind her and unhook her bra. She reacts instinctively, covering her breasts with her hands. It's a sweet, old-fashioned gesture that makes me lean forward and brush my lips over hers.

I clasp her wrists, bring her hands down, and look at her.

I feel my throat constrict.

Her breasts are perfect. Not too small. Not too large. They're—perfect. So are her nipples. They're the palest shade of pink. They look delicious and, slowly, I bend my head and lick first one and then the other.

Bailey responds as if she's touched a live electric wire. She gasps; her back arches. She gives a soft, keening cry. It's the kind of response a man wants. A total turn-on, as if I'm not already turned on way beyond anything I've ever experienced before. I run the back of my hand across her nipples. Then I feather my fingers over them; I use my thumbs and index fingers to play with the tender, lovely flesh.

Bailey is going wild and it's all I can do not to rip off our remaining clothes and plunge into her, but as badly as I want that, I want to bring her pleasure even more.

Her hand closes over mine.

It's as if she's stroking herself with me, and I hear myself groan.

How much more can either of us take?

I whisper her name. Then I bend to her, close my lips around a nipple and suck. She sobs my name. Falls back against the pillows. Her hair is like dark silk against the white linen.

"Matthew," she says brokenly. Her hips lift.

And I know the answer to my question is that I can't take much more.

I kiss her throat. Her breasts. Her belly button.

Her hands are in my hair. She's making little crooning sounds as she arches towards me. I am still kissing her. She tastes like honey. Like cream. She tastes like Bailey, and I wonder if I somehow always knew this would be the way she tastes.

I reach the place where the black silk panties kiss her skin. I ease the panties down her hips. Her thighs. Her legs.

Then, only then, I give myself permission to look at her.

There has to be a better word than beautiful to describe her.

She is everything a woman can be. Her face. Her breasts. The feminine curve of her hips.

The soft, dark curls between her thighs. How can I not kiss my way down to those curls?

I press my mouth to her belly. I go lower. Lower. Her breath hisses through her teeth. When I am almost where I need to be, she shakes her head and puts her palms flat against my chest.

"Wait," she says, "Matthew, wait—"

I can't wait. If I do, I'll die.

I clasp her hands, bring her arms above her head and kiss my way to those delicate curls. I nuzzle her. Breathe against her. I urge her to open to me and, at last, she does. I press my mouth to the petals of the pink flower her parted thighs reveal. I lick, kiss, tongue her sweet clit...

She cries out into the silent room and comes apart.

Her response shatters the last of my control. I tear off my boxers, slide my hands under her ass, lift her to me and enter her.

I shudder with the pleasure of it.

She is hot and slick. And tight. So tight.

Then she gasps. Not with pleasure. I have found a barrier...

The crazy idea that she's a virgin isn't crazy after all. My Bailey *is* a virgin. Pills or no pills, she's never been with a man before.

I go completely still.

My head spins. A virgin? I've never been with a virgin before, but I know enough to realize getting past that barrier of tender flesh will be painful. I'm going to hurt her when what I want is to pleasure her. I have to stop. Withdraw...

"Please," she sobs. "Please, please, please. Matthew. Don't stop. Don't..."

She lifts herself to me. Impales herself on me.

The world tilts.

Somehow, I manage to hold still. I can feel her

body accepting mine, adapting to the intrusion. Sweat beads my forehead. I am shaking. I wait. I wait.

Bailey moves her hips.

She moves again.

Slowly, I move forward. Very slowly. Slowly enough to kill me. One sweet inch at a time. She moans. I go very still.

"Am I hurting you, sweetheart?" I whisper.

Her eyes meet mine. Her hand cups my face. I turn my lips to the center of her palm.

"Matthew," she sighs as she lifts herself to me.

I shift my weight. I am taking her just as she is taking me. She is gasping. So am I.

And then finally, finally, I am there. I am inside her. Deep inside her. Her heat, her softness. All mine.

All mine.

At first, I am afraid to move. But my Bailey is afraid of nothing. She rocks against me. Gently. Then harder. Harder. And finally I stop thinking, stop worrying, I say her name and it has to be now.

The need to have her, take her, possess her is all I know.

I bend to her; she lifts to me. She wraps her hands around my biceps. We find a rhythm and it's perfect—but it isn't enough. I need more. I need to see her come.

I need her to surrender to me, to me, to me...

Her muscles begin to contract around my swollen dick. She sobs my name. I am driving into her. I am lost within her...

She cries out. Her body arches like a bow, and she

splinters in my arms. Then, only then, I throw back my head, I let go, and we fly into the night together.

I LIE SPRAWLED OVER HER. I outweigh her by at least seventy pounds and I know I have to move, but the world is still tilting. Finally, I lever myself away and roll to my side with her in my arms.

I feather kisses over her forehead, her cheeks, her lips. "Bailey? Honey, are you okay?"

Yeah, I know. It's the most banal after-sex question imaginable, but I have to ask. Did I hurt her? Does she have regrets? Not that I can do anything about either of those things now.

She sighs. "I'm fine."

"You sure? Because—"

She lifts her head and gives me a long, tender kiss. "Stop worrying," she says gently.

"I'm not worrying." Hell. Of course I'm worrying. I have never taken a woman's virginity before. "Do you need something?" I ask, as I go from banal to foolish. "Water? A towel? Anything?"

She laughs softly. "I need to get up, that's all."

She feathers another kiss over my lips. Then she starts to shift away and I stop her.

"Bailey? I didn't plan this. I mean, I didn't think..." *Liar!* "What I mean is, I didn't plan it. But I thought about it. About us, like this..."

She lays her hand lightly over my mouth. "So did I."

I blink. "You did?"

She blushes. "Yes. Now let me get up. I have to, you know, I have to wash up."

Reality hits. Shit. I have all the sensitivity of a bull moose. She's probably bleeding. Because of me. Because I took—

"And stop being such a male chauvinist," she says lightly. "You didn't *take* anything."

Hell. Did I say that out loud? "That's sweet of you to say, but—"

"Matthew." She rises up on her elbow. Her hair swings over the side of her face. I slide my hand into all that lovely silk and draw her to me for another kiss. "Matthew," she says, a little breathlessly, "this isn't some Victorian novel. Making love was as much my idea as yours."

I laugh and tug her down into my arms again. "What happened to my prim and proper PA?"

"You set her free," she says as she traces the outline of my mouth with the tip of her index finger.

I am delighted by her sexy confession. "Really," I say, sucking her finger into my mouth.

"Yes, really. Now, come on. Let me up. I promise, I'll be right back."

I let go of her and she rises from the bed. The chambermaid has left white velour robes on chairs on either side of the nightstands. Bailey reaches for hers, but first I get a look at her from the rear. She reminds me of an Impressionist nude. Rosy skin. Long lines. Gentle curves. Even her ass is a work of art.

I wait until she closes the bathroom door before I

check the sheets. If there's blood, I don't want her to have to deal with it. No. The sheets are pristine.

I roll onto my back, fold my arms beneath my head and stare up at the shadows dancing across the ceiling. I am not a jerk who compares making love with one woman to making love with another, but there's no escaping the fact that this was...

Incredible.

Man. It was amazing—but as amazing as it was, now what? I have gone from being my PA's boss to being her lover. And one of the basic rules in business is that you don't sleep with someone who works for you.

The realization wipes the smile from my face.

Coop warned me of where this was heading. So did Casey. I warned myself, for Christ's sake. Despite all of that, here I am, lying in a bed that bears the scents of sex and woman, waiting for Bailey to come back so we can make love—and what's with the *making love* thing? We fucked, is what we did.

And we'll do it again.

Why not?

I don't have statistics to back me, but I'm damn sure that the Basic Rule thing gets ignored a lot. You just have to set the right parameters...

The right parameters?

What in hell does that mean? What will it mean once we're back in the real world? If she won't even address me as Matthew in the office, she's sure as hell not going to want to do anything like this. I know my Bailey. She'll have rules. No fucking before noon. No fucking on my desk and, hell, the very thought of bending her over that gleaming glass surface, pulling down her panties and taking her while life outside my locked door goes on its humdrum way has me turning hard again.

Okay. The thing to do is end this now. Get up. Tell Bailey this was great, but it was a mistake...

The bathroom door opens. In the second before she switches off the light, Bailey stands silhouetted in the doorway, the white robe untied and framing her body.

Everything logical drains from my head.

Or maybe everything logical rushes into it.

This isn't about fucking or about figuring out the rules. It's about being with this woman...

"Matthew?"

I sit up against the pillows, hold out my arms, and she hurries across the floor, straight into them.

I stroke the curls back from her forehead.

"Are you all right?" I ask softly.

"Yes," she replies, and within a few seconds' time, I know that she is all right, indeed.

SHE ASKS ABOUT MY TATTOOS. Traces them with her finger.

I don't really talk much about the tatts. I had them done when I was straight out of college, still trying to figure out who I was and how I fit into the world— something it took me a while to do.

But this is different.

Bailey already knows how I went into a profession it turned out I hated. She knows endless stuff about me, so I tell her about Kathmandu. How Coop and I took six months to backpack our way through India, Nepal, Kenya and half a dozen other places and how Nepal was the one where I began to see life more clearly.

"Not clearly enough to turn down that Wall Street job," I say, as I play with her hair. "But enough to learn things."

She smiles. "Things?"

"Uh huh."

I consider telling her about mindfulness. Joyfulness. But she's gone back to tracing my tatts, this time with little kisses. She starts at my wrist and works her way up my arm, across my shoulder, and she keeps going when she gets to my chest, even though I'm not tattooed there, and I don't want her to stop kissing and touching and...

"Bailey," I whisper, and we forget about tattoos and trips and lose ourselves in each other again.

WE SLEEP, she in my arms, the sheet and comforter drawn over us. We sleep for hours and when I wake, pale gray light is poking through the sheer ivory curtains. Rain is pattering against the windows.

Bailey is still in my arms.

She's lying with her head cradled on my shoulder,

one leg high over mine. Her hand lies over my heart. Her breathing is deep and even. I want to kiss her, but I know I should let her sleep.

Liar.

I want to do more than kiss her.

We've made love three times and my dick is standing straight up again. Yes, it's the way it usually begins the day—that famous male-salute-to-the-morning thing—but this is more than that. This is me, wanting to return to Bailey's silken warmth; it's me, wanting to hear her sweet voice chanting my name as she comes.

Okay. I won't disturb her.

I'll just—I'll just ease her onto her back. Lower my mouth to hers. Kiss her. Nip gently at that luscious bottom lip. Kiss her throat. Her breasts because, hey, somehow the sheet and comforter have slipped down just enough to bare them...

Her arms rise and loop around my neck. Her eyes open; her lips curve in a smile.

"Good morning," she says softly.

"Good morning. Did you sleep well?"

"Mmm." She stretches, which is the right thing to do because she shifts her weight just enough to bring her body fully against mine. She feels my erection— the way it's responding, she'd have to be on another continent not to—and her smile turns to one of to artful innocence. "And what, exactly, is that?"

I move against her. "This?" I say innocently.

"Uh huh. That."

"It's a present."

Bailey bats her lashes. Amazing. The night has turned my virgin into a temptress.

"For me?"

"For me too."

"A present for both of us? I don't understand." She understands, all right. I love that she's teasing me, that her voice has gotten a little hoarse.

"Well," I say, "let me see if I can show you."

I move again. She makes a soft, sexy sound and her thighs fall open. I rise to my knees.

Her clit is pink and delicate and waiting for my touch, and I oblige. I take my dick in my hand, lean forward and rub the head of it up and down, up and down, slowly, slowly against her.

Her eyes darken; she catches her breath.

"We can do this," I tell her. "Unless you don't like it," I say and I start to pull back.

Bailey wraps her legs around me.

"You're a cruel man, Matthew O'Malley," she whispers. "Trying to keep that present all for yourself."

I laugh.

Then I stop laughing. I bend down and claim her mouth, and I slide into her, into all that welcoming heat and silky dampness, and we don't do anymore talking for a long, long time.

THE RAIN IS DETERMINED to spoil Vigilant Violet's plans for the day.

She's had the hours between now and the wedding

all worked out. Meals and activities at the country club. Bailey is reading the info to me from what looks like a timetable embossed with the names of the bride and groom as well as that golden dove.

Today, he isn't winking. He's smiling. So am I. My girl is sitting cross-legged in the center of our bed, snug within my encircling arms.

"Let's see," she says. "It's, what, ten o'clock?"

"Mmm," I say, nuzzling a loop of curls away from her throat. Her skin is warm and fragrant from the bath we took a little while ago in that soaking tub. No actual sex that time. My Bailey is a little sore, so I introduced her to what a creative couple can do with hands and fingers, mouths and tongues.

She turns out to be a wonderfully fast learner.

"So we've already missed breakfast. Or—" Her tone goes all dramatic and she takes on a French accent. "Or, *Monsieur*, perhaps I should say we have missed *Le Petit Déjeuner*."

"You're joking."

She lifts the page and holds it up so I can read it. "Nope. The meals—breakfast, lunch, dinner—are all listed in French."

"Because?"

"Because Vi wants it that way, I guess."

"Is she French?"

Bailey laughs.

"Is Chester?"

She laughs again. I laugh too, even as I reach under the shirt she's wearing—my shirt, unbuttoned—and cup her breasts.

"What about these, *mademoiselle*? Are these French?"

She leans her head back against my shoulder. "I love when you do that," she murmurs as I feather my thumbs over her nipples.

"And a very good thing you do," I say, kissing the side of her throat, "because I love doing it."

She tilts her face up to mine and we kiss. It's a long kiss, and wonderfully tender. In fact, everything about the last hour has been tender. The way I hold her. The way I kiss her. The way she smiles at me. Touches me. Have I ever shared so many tender moments with a woman before? Have I ever shared moments I'd describe as tender at all?

I don't think so, and the knowledge rocks me.

It also scares the crap out of me, and a little voice in my head starts telling me it's probably time to get out of this bed, out of this room, and join the real world.

"So," I say briskly, "what were the *If it rains* plans for this morning? Knowing your cousin, I'm sure there were some."

"Well, people were on their own for breakfast."

I nod. "Find the local McD's and chow down."

Bailey laughs. "Or something."

That's what we did. The *or something* part. It's why we should get out of here now. I start to suggest that. Instead, I hear myself ask about lunch.

"Rain alternative," she says. "Meet at the clubhouse. Have lunch in the dining room."

"Excellent idea. Lunch at the clubhouse."

Bailey turns in my arms. She drops the schedule

and puts her arms around my neck. "Actually, it really is an excellent idea. I don't know about you, but I'm starved."

I am too, but with Bailey looking up at me, her eyes glittering, her lips curved in a soft smile, the plan to get out and mingle loses appeal.

"Or," I say, "we could stay right where we are. Order in."

"The inn doesn't have a kitchen."

I tip her face up. "We passed a famous Italian restaurant on our way here yesterday."

She wrinkles her brow. "A famous Italian restaurant? Are you sure?"

"Am I sure, the woman asks. Of course I'm sure. It was a little place, right on Main Street. Dom-Een-Oh's."

"DomEen...?" Bailey laughs. "Domino's."

I grin as I lean my forehead against hers. "Garlic? Black olives? Extra cheese?"

"And broccoli."

Jesus. Broccoli? I smile and manage to repress a shudder. "*Oui, mademoiselle*. I was going to ask for snails, but broh-coh-lee is better."

"I thought this was an Italian restaurant, *monsieur*."

I GRIN. "Italian, French, what's the difference?"

"You're right. But no snails. I've always preferred frog's legs on my pizza," she says. Then she rolls her eyes, jabs her finger at her open mouth and makes the most impressive gagging sounds I've heard since sixth grade.

In the end, she takes pity on me, maybe because she's sitting in my lap when I phone in our order and she sees the look on my face as I start to say "broccoli."

"Forget the broccoli," she whispers, and I take time out of placing the order to drop a quick kiss on her lips.

The pizza arrives. We open the champagne we never got to last night, we eat in bed, and it's more of a feast than good old Violet and the best chef in Paris could ever have concocted.

15

The rain stops in mid-afternoon.

We shower. And, yes, we find a way to put that marble bench in the shower stall to excellent use. Then I put on jeans, a pale blue shirt with a button-down collar and the sleeves rolled up, and my roper boots. Bailey slips into a pair of jeans that make the most of her delectable hips and ass, tops the jeans with a floaty silver thing, and puts on another pair of mules. These are silver. Or maybe gray. Whatever you call them, they're the perfect finishing touch.

She looks sexy enough for Manhattan and casual enough for a country club, which is where we're heading.

Tea on the lawn at 3:30, the schedule reads, though we figure that has to be problematic considering all the rain.

Wrong.

The grass is soaked, but the tea party is still on.

A couple of steps and Bailey's spiked heels sink into

the ground like tent stakes the time my Scout troupe went camping too close to a New Jersey swamp. It's happening to all the other women; the lawn is dotted with females staggering from one spot to another.

Not my woman.

Bailey clings to my arm, leans down and yanks off the mules. Then she plants her bare feet in the soggy soil, roll her cuffs to mid-calf, looks at me and laughs.

"So much for being fashionable," she says.

What she is, is cute as hell. The staggerers seem to agree because it only takes a few minutes before they eyeball her, dump their fancy shoes and squish their way through the grass the same as she's doing.

I tuck her shoes into the back pockets of my jeans. Then I take her hand and we head for today's buffet line. This time we're both hungry. The pizza was good, but we've been blowing through lots of calories.

"Time to refuel," I say as I hand her a plate, and Bailey does that batting-her-lashes bit and says she definitely wants me to keep my energy levels up.

How could I not have known the woman who's worked for me all these years?

Long tables offer up an assortment of goodies, though I suspect this isn't the kind of tea somebody from England would recognize. There are plenty of little cakes and tiny crustless sandwiches, but there's also real food and despite all the fancy French names, it's pretty basically American. There's a guy at a grill turning out burgers and hot dogs, another plucking lobster tails from an enormous kettle. I half expect Bailey to ask the pedigree of the burgers and dogs, but she doesn't. Turns out the grill guy is also doing a stack of hockey pucks labeled Vegetarian, and that's what she chooses.

"That way I don't have to wonder about the meat," she tells me, her expression earnest and caring and, what the hell, I make the same choice. But we also take lobster tails after Bailey and the server with the kettle and the tongs sees the hockey puck on her plate. "Harvested off the Maine coast," he confides, "from carefully managed, environmentally sound waters."

She thanks him. I do too, because not eating lobster when I know a lobster would happily eat me if our situations were reversed is not high on my list of Doing the Right Thing...Except, I realize as we look for a table, I would have done it to keep my woman happy —and what is with this *my woman* stuff? I am not a guy who thinks that way. I don't believe in absolutist language. A woman belongs to herself, same as a dude belongs to himself...

"Bailey? Come sit with us."

Shit. The bride has spotted us. She and the groom are at a table for four, and she's beaming the kind of smile you see in toothpaste ads. Big, bright, and phony.

I take Bailey's hand and dip my head to hers. "Your choice, babe," I murmur.

"We'd love to," my girl says, and the only way I know she's lying is because she squeezes my hand hard enough so her nails dig into my palm.

We join the happy couple.

Elevator Boy starts things off by saying he's pissed that there was nothing the country club could do about the weather. It's hard not to go all wide-eyed and say *Well, duh,* but I manage. Violet the Vixen—that's the role she's dressed for in a clingy knit top cut so low I'm amazed her toes aren't showing and black tights that I suspect make it tough for her to breathe—Violet says they decided to hold the tea outside anyway. Elevator Boy says they didn't have a choice because the dining room was already booked. Violet shoots him a look and says he really should have told the manager how he felt about that. Elevator Boy says he did. Violet says he should have made his position on the matter more determined.

After that, they fall silent.

I clear my throat. "So," I say brightly, "where are you two going on your honeymoon?"

"Greece," Elevator Boy says.

"Chester rented a yacht."

Elevator Boy swallows. The sound is audible.

"I rented a nice boat," he says.

"A yacht," Violet clarifies.

He leans towards her. "It's a boat. A very nice boat."

Her eyes narrow. I told you they were narrow to begin with, remember? Well, now they're just little slits.

"I thought you chose the yacht."

Chester swallows again. "This weekend," he says, "the party, the wedding..." He throws me a beseeching look. "You're in business Mark, right?"

"It's Matt. And yes. Yes, I am."

"I bet you understand cash flow issues."

What I understand is that the guy I envision as

Napoleon standing in an elevator with a box of detergent clutched to his chest has probably blown a small fortune to please his almost-wife.

I also understand that I want no part of a bloodletting.

Bailey's hand is still in mine. I give it a little squeeze that means *Please, let's get the fuck out of here.* She gives me a little squeeze in return, but it means *Hey, I'm just starting to have fun.*

"Actually," she says, "Matthew never has cash flow problems."

"No?"

"No." Her smile would do the Mona Lisa proud. "But then, Matthew has a degree in finance." She looks at Elevator Boy. "He was on The Street for several years."

The Street. It's what people who want to impress other people call Wall Street—and I have never once heard my woman use the term.

Chester—I can no long think of him as either Napoleon or Elevator Boy, not when I'm starting to feel sorry for him—looks glum. Violet looks—I'm not sure how she looks. Envious? Surprised? Angry? How about all those things rolled into one?

Bailey bites into her hockey-puck-on-a-bun and chews. "Umm. This is delicious, sweetheart. Try yours."

Sweetheart? She's talking to me. I lift the bun and chomp down.

"Good, isn't it?" I nod. For a hockey puck, it's not bad, but I abandon it in favor of the lobster. Bailey turns her smile on Chester. "Do you have a degree in business?" she asks.

Chester shakes his head. "I have launderettes," he says, so unhappily that I have to struggle against reaching across the table and patting him on the shoulder.

Okay. I'd never go that far, but I do feel bad for the guy. I mean, somebody has to own launderettes. Evidently, Bailey is starting to take pity on him too, because she changes the topic.

"So," she says, looking at Violet, "you look great."

Violet stops glaring at Chester. She turns her attention to Bailey, and suddenly I can feel something bad coming.

"Why, thank you," she simpers. "And you look—"

"Oh, I know." My girl lifts our joined hands to her lips and kisses my knuckles. "Matthew is always telling me how wonderful I look and I always point out that it's his doing." There it is. That lash-flutter thing. I can feel my gut knotting in anticipation of what comes next. "I wouldn't admit this to anyone but you, cuz, but, well, it's the sex. You know? Makes your skin glow." She giggles. It's the first time in all the years I know her that I have ever heard Bailey giggle. "Plus, it means no dieting. It helps you lose weight, then keeps you trim." Violet's mouth has formed a perfect O. Mine probably has too. Chester pretty much looks like a man fighting for his life, but Bailey's not finished. "Although," she says, with a little frown, "come to think of it, my Mom mentioned you wanted to take off a few pounds and don't get me wrong, you look fabulous, but—" She looks from Violet to Chester and back to Violet again. "You don't seem to have lost an ounce."

Holy shit.

I stare at Bailey. She flashes another beatific smile. Then she attacks her lobster tail with vengeance. The rest of us watch in silence. When she's done, she sighs, pats her lips with her napkin and looks at me.

"We'd better go," she says sweetly. "The ceremony's at—what time is it, Vi? Seven?"

"Eight," Violet the Vanquished says.

Bailey gets to her feet. So do I. She loops her arm through mine. "See you guys then," she says, and adds coyly, "We'll try not to be late."

Then we're moving across the wet lawn, heading for the parking lot. No guys in Good Humor suits this afternoon, so I don't have to make a bank withdrawal to claim my car.

"Wow," I say when we reach it.

"Wow, what?"

Her tone is pure innocence, but there's laughter in her eyes. I open her door; she slips inside the Corvette and I go around to the driver's side.

"'He was on The Street for several years,'" I say, trying—and failing—to mimic her voice.

"Well, you were."

"Did you ever hear me call it that?"

Bailey snaps her seat belt shut. "No."

I turn on the engine, step on the gas. The car moves forward.

"And the sex thing..."

"What about it?"

I look at her. She's blushing.

"I cannot believe you talked about us. Having sex."

I say it solemnly. No smile. No hint that what I really want to do is laugh.

"I didn't. I talked about sex. Its benefits. In general."

I check for traffic and turn onto the road—and suddenly, Bailey gasps. Then she makes a little moaning sound. "Ohmygod," she says. "I did, didn't I? Talked about us. Having, you know, sex..."

"The newest diet craze," I say. "By tomorrow, it'll be all over the internet. *How to Lose Weight and Keep it Off*, by Bailey Abrams."

She buries her face in her hands. "I must have lost my mind! But Violet was always so awful...Talking endlessly about boys and doing it...That's what she called sex. Doing it. And she never missed the chance to tell me I needed to lose weight."

I reach for Bailey's hand.

"You don't need to lose a thing," I tell her. "Not an ounce. And definitely not that new attitude."

"But I lied. I mean, I made it sound as if you and I have been having sex for months and months and—"

I lift her hand to my lips and kiss it. "The only lie you told was when you said we were having sex. We're making love. And there's a difference."

She stares at me.

Jesus H. Christ, if I could, I'd stare at myself. We're making love? Wasn't it just a couple of hours ago I reminded myself that what we're doing is fucking?

Okay. Words are just words. That's what my mother would say. Except my mother must never know about this. Not that I'm fucking Bailey. Shit. Of course she mustn't know that. For one thing, the last conversation my Mom and I had about sex was when I was seven and I asked her where babies came from.

For another, Mom wouldn't approve of this. Of my involvement with Bailey. Same as Coop and Casey, she'd point out that Bailey was my friend, my employee, that I would surely be stepping into a mess if I tried to pass myself off as her boyfriend no matter how valid the cause.

And she'd be right.

They were all right.

I am not just involved with Bailey, I am sleeping with her.

Fucking her.

Dammit.

I am making love with her, and when she looks at me and says, very softly, that she knows she did the wrong thing, the only way I can think of assuring her that she didn't is to get her back to the inn, out of the 'Vette, into our room and into my arms.

Because I don't give a crap what you call it.

What's happening between us in that bed and, okay, out of it, is something I'm not yet ready to define.

Or give up.

WE SHOWER AGAIN.

We get dressed.

Bailey looks spectacular. Long pale pink gown. Matching heels. Hair loose and lightly curling.

I'm in my tux. It's hand-tailored. After I moved up in the construction field I found myself attending lots of banquets and awards ceremonies. I've even won a couple of those awards. The point is, I figured that it would be sensible to own my own monkey suit instead of having to rent one and once I reached that conclusion, having one made to fit me made sense.

Bottom line?

We both look pretty damn good.

I put my arm around Bailey and draw her to the mirror. We stand before it and gaze at our reflections.

"Ms. Abrams," I say.

"Mr. O'Malley," she replies.

We smile. Then I turn her towards me and give her a soft kiss. She reaches up and adjusts my bow tie.

"Showtime," she says, only without any of the nervous anticipation of last night.

Tonight, we're going to have fun.

AND WE DO.

First, of course, we sit through the ceremony. And, despite everything, it's, you know, it's okay. I don't know if Violet and Chester wrote their own vows or if they had some help. Either way the vows are the kind people should be willing to make at the start of a marriage. The judge who marries them says some corny crap, but even that's not bad. And when Chester kisses his bride, we all applaud.

Even my Bailey.

She leans to me and whispers, "Violet looks beautiful, doesn't she?"

Well, I wouldn't go that far, but Violet looks better than she did last night or this afternoon, so I clasp Bailey's hand and say yeah, she does.

Afterwards, we line up to go through the receiving line. Bailey embraces the mother and father of the bride, she embraces Chester's folks, then Chester and, finally, Violet.

She holds Violet's hands and speaks softly to her. I am, of course, right next to Bailey so I hear every word.

"Vi," Bailey says, "I know we're cousins, but I'm sorry we were never really friends."

I'm amazed. Violet is clearly shocked, but the real shocker is when she says she's sorry too.

Bailey smiles and hugs her. "I just know you'll have a wonderful honeymoon with Chester, and a long and happy life."

Violet's eyes tear up. Chester's been eavesdropping and now he yanks his handkerchief from his pocket and hands it to his bride.

"Thank you, Bailey," Vi says.

Chester and I exchange a quick smile. "Congratulations, man," I say.

"Thank you. And when Violet and I get back...Can I call you? Take you to lunch? Ask you a few questions about, you know, my business?"

I think of telling him I don't know jackshit about washers and dryers, but this isn't a time for that.

"Sure," I say, and he grins and pumps my hand.

So all is well. Bailey has faced her demons. Violet has shown she has a human side...

Maybe not.

"We'll get together when Chester and I get home from Greece," Vi tells Bailey. "I'll take you to my hairdresser. I'm sure he can do something with that mane of yours. Not that the way you wear it doesn't have a certain, you know, Nature Girl charm."

Her smile would put a diabetic into a coma.

Bailey draws back. It's barely perceptible, but I can see it and I prepare for the worst.

The worst doesn't come.

Instead, my girl smiles. "Thank you," she says pleasantly, "but I like my hair just the way it is."

"Oh," Violet says, and the conversation ends because I put my arm around Bailey and lead her into the ballroom.

No buffet this time, just a lot of formally dressed tables. A ten-piece band is playing a credible cover of an old tune, *While My Guitar Gently Weeps*. I'm not sure it's wedding music, but I've always liked it and I draw Bailey close.

"You were wonderful," I tell her quietly.

She looks at me. "Really?"

"Yeah." What I want to tell her is that she's always wonderful, but I sweep her into my arms and out onto the dance floor.

THE EVENING PASSES QUICKLY. And yes, we have a good time.

We're seated at a table with a bunch of cousins and they turn out to be nice people. We laugh and drink champagne—the real stuff this time. And we dance a lot. Bailey thinks she can't dance, but once she relaxes and lets go, she's fine.

Besides, I don't really want to dance.

I just want to hold her in my arms and sway to the music.

Everything is going just fine. This whole weekend was about helping Bailey find her wings and it's turned out to be more than that. It's turned out to be—special. Hell. There has to be a better way to describe it. Not just what's happened in bed. The rest of it. We're having fun. Enjoying being together. Bailey is blossoming, and I'm not foolish enough to think it's because of me.

I'm simply fortunate enough to be watching a woman come into her own.

And, in a way, so am I.

The past couple of days have been, I don't know, a kind of exploration of myself and my life. I guess this is mindfulness, maybe even joyfulness. The realization puts a prickly sensation on the nape of my neck, kind of the way you might feel standing in the doorway of a dark room, trying to decide if you're frightened or excited by what 's ahead. It's pretty much what the monks told us would happen at some point in our lives, Coop's and mine, if we let it. I always thought my moment had come when I realized being in finance wasn't for me, but now I start to wonder if it might be something more than that...

And then it all comes to a screeching halt.

Bailey and I are alone at our table. Everybody has abandoned us in favor of the dessert carts that have just been wheeled in, meaning these are our first few moments alone in what seems like hours, and we are making the most of this quiet time together.

I've pulled my chair against hers. My arm is around her and her head is on my shoulder. We're talking about things. Nothing important. Just things, the way people do when they're comfortable together. I've just said something about who-knows-what, certainly nothing urgent or brilliant, but she's listening to every word with her face turned up to mine and a sweet smile on her lips. It's so sweet that I kiss her. It's a demure kiss, the kind that's okay in public, but then I run my hand over her shoulder and into her hair, and she sighs and I kiss her again...

That's when a woman's voice screeches my name.

"Matthew O'Malley! Matty, it really is you!"

Bailey jerks away as a hand lands hard on my shoulder and waves of perfume envelop us. I look up, but I already know who it is. The perfume, the screechy voice, the Matty.

Nobody's called me that since I was maybe nine or ten...

Except for Jessica Simms.

I look up and yes, holy crap, there she is. My mother's friend. No. Not at friend, exactly. A neighbor. Okay, she's more of an acquaintance.

Fuck.

What she is, is a pain in the ass. She's the world biggest gossip, so if you figure she's the worst person Bailey and I could run into this weekend, you just scored one hundred percent, because if you also figure I have no intention of mentioning this weekend to anyone, you're right.

Certainly not to my mom.

And there's not chance in a million Mom won't find out about it now.

Which is not good.

See, Mom knows Bailey. She likes her. A lot. She's always asking after her. I've heard her muse over why a girl like Bailey is still single. At one point a couple of years back, Mom even ran this little campaign that involved telling me how terrific Bailey was, how some man would be incredibly lucky to find her, and after a while I'd started to think—hint hint—that maybe I was supposed to be that man. The idea had seemed so ludicrous that I hadn't even bothered telling my mother there was no way I'd ever be interested in Bailey as a woman...

"Matty? Aren't you going to say hello?"

I rise to my feet, take a deep breath and, I hope, smile.

"Mrs. Simms. What a surprise."

She beams at me. "For me too. I had no idea you'd be here."

"No. Well, it was—it was sort of last minute..."

"Aren't you going to introduce me to your friend?"

You can almost see the word *friend* blinking on and off in neon.

"Oh. Sorry. This is Bailey. Bailey Abrams. Bailey, this is my parents' neighbor. Jessica Simms."

"Neighbor," Jessica Simms says with a roll of her eyes. "I'm his mother's best friend."

Bailey stands up and holds out her hand. Mrs. Simms takes it. She's also taking in everything else about Bailey, from the top of her head to the tips of her toes.

"It's nice to meet you," Bailey says.

"Oh, believe me, Miss Abrams, it's a pleasure to meet you!"

"Call me Bailey, please," Bailey says.

She's smiling, but she glances at me. I can read the question she's asking. *Is this bad?* I try to look at her in a way that says it's nothing to worry about, but I don't think I do a very good job of delivering the message.

"Well," Mrs. Simms says, "why don't we all sit down?"

I pull out a chair for her and she plops into it. Once we're all seated, she beams at me.

"So what are you doing here, Matty? Is the groom —my nephew—a business acquaintance of yours?" She looks at Bailey. "Chester owns a big dry cleaning business," she confides.

That Bailey doesn't correct her about Elevator Boy's profession is the first hint I get that she's as concerned about this situation as I am.

"And who are you related to, my dear? Well, silly

me. The bride, of course, because I'd know you if you and the groom were relatives."

"I'm the bride's cousin."

"Ah. Violet. A charming girl who's made an excellent catch." Mrs. Simms winks. "But you've made the better catch. Our Matty here might as well be called the Bachelor of the Year."

"Oh," Bailey says quickly, "Matthew isn't...I mean, Matthew and I..."

"We work together," I say. Bailey flinches. "What I mean is, we're friends." Another flinch. What the hell, I go for broke. "Very good friends."

Mrs. Simms laughs. I'm not trying to be cruel when I say her laugh has always reminded me of a horse's whinny. In the past I found that kind of amusing. Right now, nothing is amusing. I can absolutely, positively, no-doubt-about-it see where this is heading.

"An understatement," she says. "I can't believe your mother didn't tell me!"

"Tell you...?"

"You know, Matty. That you were seeing somebody. She must be thrilled! Every mother wants to see her son find the right girl and settle down."

Bailey casts me a pleading look, but I can't come up with anything that will dig us out of this.

"I thought I'd spotted you. And right then, Chester and his lovely bride came by our table to say hello and I asked if I was right and my dear friend's son, Matthew O'Malley, was a guest tonight and the bride said yes, he was, he was here with his fiancée..."

I lose the thread of conversation for a couple of

seconds as I contemplate how you'd manage strangling someone discreetly when you're in a room with a couple of hundred people.

"You know," Mrs. Simms says with a sly smile, "while I was watching you two, I wondered how often it must happen."

"How often what must happen?" I croak.

"You know, Matty. A young couple in love goes to a wedding and, wallah, before you know it they're planning a wedding of their own."

She just said *wallah* when what she meant was *voila*. I've heard other people do that. Normally, it drives me whacko—my mom's DNA at work—but right now I'm whacko enough without worrying about Jessica Simms fucking up French and English.

"That's the thing," I say. "See, Bailey and I aren't—"

"You aren't ready to talk about it yet. I understand. I'll be our little secret."

Meaning the inhabitants of Drury Drive for two miles in an ever-expanding circumference will hear news of the impending nuptials of Matthew O'Malley and Bailey Abrams by tomorrow lunchtime, the latest.

I want to protest, but what would I say? *The truth*, a little voice in my head whispers, but the truth is complicated and involved and...

And—and I can't do that.

The truth is too messy. It would hurt Bailey, and hurting her is the last thing I'd ever want to do.

We get through another few minutes. Bailey and I are silent while Jessica Simms berates the Beef Wellington for being half raw and the chicken for being overcooked.

At last, mercifully, she gets to her feet. We rise too, and she hugs us both, wishes us well, gives that whinny of a laugh as she prepares to gallop off to another pasture. She says she can't wait to talk to my mother and tell her how happy she is that someone's finally caught me...

She leaves. I run my hand through my hair. "Wow," I say. "Who'd have expected..."

"Yes," Bailey says. "Who'd have expected."

Bailey's voice is low. Her face is pale. She looks the way I feel.

"Hey," I say softly. "You okay?"

"I'm fine."

She's not. I can tell. And, idiot that I am, I figure I can improve things by making light of what just happened.

"Well," I say brightly, "I'm in for an interesting phone call from my mother."

Bailey swallows hard. I know because I can see her throat constrict as she reaches for her purse.

"It's late," she says. "I'd like to leave."

"Honey. Don't let that woman spoil things. She's just a busybody."

"A busybody with news she can't wait to spread."

Bailey starts to move back her chair. I clasp her wrist.

"She saw us here together. So what? You were going to a wedding. You needed a—What's it called?"

"A plus one." Bailey looks at me. "But she saw you acting as a lot more than my date, Matthew. She saw us, you know, together."

Kissing, is what she means. Touching.

"And then my stupid cousin told her we were engaged." Her eyes flash. "I'll bet Violet did it deliberately. To stir up trouble."

"This is one time Violet's probably innocent of any wrongdoing. She's seen us the way you just said. Together. Maybe she, you know, jumped to conclusions."

"Is it impossible for you to construct a sentence without saying 'you know'?"

Whoa. Bailey said the first *you know.* I'm only responsible for the second one. My girl is angry. But at me? What have I done?

"Look, sweetheart—"

"I am not your sweetheart."

Dammit. This is going downhill fast.

"Bailey. Calm down."

"I am absolutely calm."

The hell she is. Still, confused as I am, I know better than to contradict her. Instead, I link our fingers together.

"Is it a problem? Violet—" The phrase *you know* is on my lips Fortunately, I catch myself just in time. "Violet thinking we're engaged?"

"Is it a..." She pulls her hand from mine. "Of course it's a problem. Bad enough I let people believe you were my date. My boyfriend. By the time tonight is over, everybody will believe you and I are getting married." She shakes her head. "I cannot, I *cannot* believe I thought this would work!"

She's upset. I'm baffled. "Yeah, but it *did* work. Didn't you just say that?"

"Don't be an idiot, Matthew! Violet will make sure the real story gets out. That this was all a sham." She buries her face in her hands. "My mother's going to be horrified."

"Honey..."

She looks up. There's fire in her eyes. "Do not call me that."

I can feel the situation snowballing. There must be something I can do to stop it, but I'll be damned if I can think of what it is. Plus, dancing around in the back of my head is what faces me unless I get to my mother before Jessie Simms does. Mom will go from joy that I've finally come to my senses to dismay that I haven't in less time than it takes to blink.

Bailey shakes her head. "I should have known this wouldn't work!"

"But it did. Everybody who saw us believes we really are a couple."

"You mean, we were excellent actors."

"Right!"

Her cheeks flame. Her mouth thins. She's either going to slug me or kill me and as soon as I realize how that idiotic *Right!* must have sounded, I know I can't blame her if she does either, but what she does instead is snatch her purse from the table, shoot to her feet and head for the ballroom exit.

"Bailey. Wait!"

I am fast, but she's picked up the pace. She's all but

running and now I am too—and, of course, people are craning their necks to watch the show.

Violet and Chester loom up in front of me.

"Everything okay?" Violet purrs. "Oh, and by the way, you two put on a great act."

In an instant it all comes together. Bailey was right. Violet did deliberately tell people we're engaged. Then all she had to do was wait for the hammer to fall.

Bailey's not going to get even with her cousin, she's going to be humiliated.

I have never hit a woman in my life. Never even imagined wanting to. Right now, it takes all that's in me not to nail Vicious Violet right on the chin.

Instead, I look at Chester. The expression on his face is pretty much a synonym for confused.

"It's not too late," I tell him. "Do yourself a favor and walk away before it gets worse."

Then I take off and barrel through the place until I'm out the front door.

At first I don't see Bailey.

Then I do.

It's raining again and she's standing right out in it, except this isn't simply rain, it's a deluge. She's already soaked. One of the parking attendants runs up with an umbrella, but she waves him off.

"All I need is a taxi," I hear her say.

"She doesn't need a taxi," I tell the kid. I hand him my parking stub and a fifty. "The red Corvette," I snap. "And make it fast." Then I whip off my tux jacket and wrap it around Bailey. She tries to shove it away, but I won't let her. I hang onto her until the kid pulls up in my car. He gets out, comes around to the passenger side and opens the door. Bailey doesn't move and I grab her and damn near stuff her into the seat. Then I slam the door, run around to the driver's side and get behind the wheel.

We pull out of the driveway and onto the road.

"What kind of stunt was that?" I demand. "You want to get pneumonia?"

"What you mean is, did I want to spoil the act?"

I take my eyes off the rain-slicked road long enough to glare at her.

"You're being ridiculous."

She lifts her chin and folds her arms over her chest. "At least you're not trying to deny it."

"Deny what?" I say, if only to give myself time to think because I know damn well what she's talking about.

"Are you sure you were a finance major? Because you missed your calling, Mr. O'Malley. You should have gone on the stage."

Jesus!

"Bailey. That's not fair."

"You're right. It's not. I was the one who started this."

"You didn't start anything. I offered to come with you this weekend, remember?"

"You offered to pretend to be my boyfriend, but only because you heard me tell my mother a lie about having a boyfriend in the first place."

"Let's not play Who Said What When, okay?" I shoot another look at her. Shit. She's shaking. I reach out and turn on the heat. "Pull the jacket around you."

"Don't give me orders."

"I'm not giving your orders. I'm trying to keep you from getting sick. Pull the fucking jacket around you."

"There's no need to curse."

"Goddammit!," I snarl.

And then I shut up.

The next time I look over, Bailey is still sitting bolt upright but at least she's drawn my jacket close around her.

"Look," I say, "this will all blow over."

Bailey's laugh is not a jocular sound.

It is only later, when I replay this conversation in my head for the thousandth time, that I realize how truly stupid I was to say such a thing. At this moment, however, it strikes me as a way to calm her.

Evidently not.

"I wanted to get even with Violet," she says. "Instead, I'm never going to be able to face her again. And my mother...When she finds out we were only pretending..."

My thoughts skitter back to *my* mother. By the time I get to her, she'll have rented a hall, hired a band and ordered flowers.

"Okay," I say, "all right. This is going to be a little more complicated then we figured...Hey!" Bailey has punched me in the arm. "Watch that! You want us to skid?"

"I want never to have laid eyes on you, Matthew O'Malley. That's what I want. We made—*I* made a spectacle of myself in front of all those people. How come I didn't realize that was what would happen?"

Here we go again. She means the kissing. The touching. The being focused on each other whether we were dancing or talking or just sitting side by side.

"We didn't do anything two people who enjoy being together wouldn't do."

"We appeared...intimate."

The anger has drained from her voice. That should be a good sign. Somehow, it isn't.

She is silent as we turn off the main road and head for our inn. In fact she is silent until we're parked outside the place. Then she says, in a tremulous whisper, "We *were* intimate."

My gut knots. I don't want her to regret the hours we spent in bed, in each other's arms; I don't want her to regret our making love all through the night and through the day.

I don't want her to regret the precious gift she gave me.

I turn off the engine and turn to her. I reach for her, but she pulls back.

"Bailey," I say softly, "we didn't do anything wrong. We made love, and making love is a good thing."

She has stopped shaking. That, at least, is positive. But the way she avoids looking at me and instead studies her hands, which are folded in her lap...

Not so positive.

"We lied," she says softly.

I almost deny that, but how can I? We *did* lie when we let people think we were a couple.

"*I* lied," she says, even more softly.

I take her hands in mine. "We both did."

She bends her head. Her hair, rain-soaked and tangled, falls around her face.

"My lie was worse."

Okay. I'm sure I know what she means. She lied to her mother. She figures that makes hers the bigger lie. But it was a game. Make believe. And in a good cause.

"Matthew?"

"Yes?"

"I'd like to go home now."

"We are home, honey. We pulled into the driveway five minutes ago."

She looks at me. "Home," she says. "To the city."

"You mean, you want to go back to Manhattan?"

She nods. "Yes."

It's almost midnight. The rain is coming down so hard I wouldn't be surprised to see an ark sail past.

I think of the big bed waiting in our suite. The fire in the fireplace. I think of undressing my woman, taking her to that big bed and warming her with my body...

"Please," she whispers.

I nod. Somehow, I know she doesn't want to go inside the inn at all. I lean over, kiss the tip of her nose.

"I'll be right back," I say.

I use the inn's key to unlock the front door. The lobby is empty. I run up the stairs to our room, open the door, step inside and look around.

I don't want to be here either, not without Bailey.

I find a pen and pad beside the telephone and

scribble a note asking if someone would be so kind as to pack our things and ship them to my address. It's an emergency, I add. There's a soft woolen afghan draped over the back of the loveseat that stands before the fire and I write that management should add the cost of the little blanket to my bill, along with charges for packing and shipping.

I sign my name, leave the keys and a fifty on top of the note—it's a good weekend for spare fifties, I think with a sudden tightness in my throat. Then I pick up the afghan and hurry down to the car.

Bailey is sitting as I left her, hands folded, eyes fixed on the rain-flooded windshield.

"Hey," I say softly as I open her door. I drape the afghan over her. "We'll be home in no time. Why don't you close your eyes and get some sleep?"

We are home in just a little more than no time.

I don't know if she sleeps or not, only that she keeps her face turned away and she doesn't speak. When I pull up in front of her apartment building, I shut off the car and turn towards her.

She is pushing the blanket aside.

"I'm coming up with you," I say.

She looks at me and puts her hand on my arm. "I'm fine."

"Bailey. Everything about this weekend was wonderful. Being with you. Making love with you. Being happy together. None of that was a lie. Will you remember that?"

She leans in and cups my face with her hands.

"You were never the liar, Matthew," she says quietly. "It was always me."

Then she kisses me. It's a soft kiss, the mere whisper of her lips against mine, and the sad sweetness of it almost undoes me.

"No," I say. "Wait..."

Her door opens. Shuts. She runs to her building...

And just that quickly, I am alone.

16

I spend Sunday in a funk.

I leaf through the Sports section of the Sunday New York Times, but after I toss it aside I can't recall anything I read.

I watch football, but I have no idea who wins or loses the games.

I phone out for a pizza. Walter hears me say the word when I place the order. "Woof," he says happily, and starts slobbering. When the pizza arrives, I look at it, remember the pizza Bailey and I shared just yesterday, and suddenly my appetite is gone.

Walter lucks out.

Instead of sharing the pie with me, he gets all of it.

I consider calling my folks. Sooner or later, I have to deal with Mrs. Simmons and what she's eager to tell my mother, but I revert to what I did when I was in trouble as a kid. I put off with the problem in hopes it will go away. After a while, when my mother doesn't call me, I decide it *has* gone away.

Pathetic, right?

And, of course, I try phoning Bailey.

My calls go to voice mail each and every time.

I leave messages that range from light-hearted —*Hey, the Patriots are playing the Jets. How about I come by and we laugh at what New York calls football?* all the way to pleading—*Bailey. I never meant for you to get hurt. Please pick up. We have to talk.*

In mid-afternoon, my phone rings. I forget such niceties as Caller ID and grab the phone.

"Bailey?"

"Matt. This is your mother."

I bite back a groan. "Mom. Look, if this is about the weekend..."

It's about the weekend, all right. And me. And Bailey, and what a wonderful girl she is and how I made her cry by pretending I cared for her and how could I ever have treated her so badly...

And, and, and.

It's clear that my mother has heard a garbled version of what happened. I wait until she runs out of breath. Then I tell her the truth. Well, most of it. How Bailey's been mistreated all her life by her cousin. How she just couldn't face turning up at that cousin's wedding without a date.

How I offered to help.

The only thing I don't tell her is that Bailey and I spent most of the weekend in bed,. That's much too private. Besides, it wasn't part of the plan and the truth is, I don't regret it.

Making love with Bailey was...It was incredible. I

am not going to talk about it with anyone, and I sure as hell am not going to forget it.

"Matt?"

"Yeah. I'm here."

"Bailey is one in a million."

I agree.

"I know you meant well, son, but you should have realized this scheme would backfire."

I rub my forehead. "I didn't think it would or I'd never have suggested it."

My mother sighs. "Didn't you know Bailey had feelings for you?"

"Mom. You're reading stuff into this."

"Matt, I love you—but like all men, you're dense when it comes to women."

That hurts. I pride myself on my relationships with my mother and my sister.

"Not with your sister and me," my mother says. Did I mention she's good at mind-reading? "You just don't think like a woman."

How can I argue with that?

"You don't see into them. And before you tell me I'm wrong, let me clarify my meaning."

Jesus. Mom's in teaching mode. If it's possible, things are about to go from bad to worse.

"I'm sure you can tell when a woman is trying to impress you. Or turn your head. But when it comes to reading a real woman's real emotions..."

"Mom. Do us both a favor. Just say it, okay?"

My mother sighs. "There's no artifice about Bailey, son. What you see is what you get."

"I know that."

"She has feelings for you, Matt. Deep feelings."

That's ridiculous. It's drama-laden. It's overblown. It's typically female...

If you knew anything at all about me, you'd know I've wanted you forever.

I blink. I can hear Bailey saying those words as if she were in the room with me.

Yeah, but we were talking about sex. About fucking.

"Matt?" Mom's voice softens. "I'm sorry things turned out the way they did."

"Yeah. Me, too."

After the call ends I realize how bad things really are. What I should have said was *So am I*, but I didn't. And my mother didn't correct me.

Shit.

I reach for the phone to try to call Bailey her again, but it rings. This time, I glance at the caller ID.

It's my sister.

Better to take the call or not?

Or not.

Four rings, and it goes to voice mail. "Matt, you big fat turd..."

Man. News travels fast.

Casey finishes leaving her sisterly message. And the damn phone rings again.

It's Coop. I decide to play it safe and let him go to voice mail too.

"Hey, dude," he says cheerfully, "I hear your weekend bombed." He chuckles. "I can almost hear you saying 'How does he know that?' Well, you remember my cousin Shirley? Her brother-in-law plays cards with a guy named Simms and Simms has an aunt Jessica..." Coop's tone softens. "Dude. You need a shoulder, gimme a call."

I need more than a shoulder. I need a payloader to dig out from the mess I've made. Not for me. For Bailey. I'll deal with the gossip, but I can't stand by and let her get hurt.

I call her.

No answer, of course.

The message I leave is half plea, half demand. I tell her she has to talk to me. That we're not going to leave things this way. When she doesn't pick up or respond I grab my jacket. I'm going to go uptown and—

And what?

Bang on her door? Camp outside it?

I toss the jacket aside and slump down on the sofa. Walter jumps up and crams himself into the too-small space next to me. He jams his muzzle into my armpit and whines.

I rub his ears.

"I know," I say. "But maybe what she needs is time to herself."

And I'll give it to her—until I get to the office tomorrow morning.

I GET to the office an hour earlier than usual. Everybody else comes in at nine. Not Bailey. She's not due in at eight, but that's when she prefers to get there.

Except, she isn't. She isn't there.

Yes—but is there a faint scent of lemon in the air?

"Bailey?" I hurry through the place, checking as I go. The copy room. The accounting office. The design studio. The conference room. There's no sign of Bailey, but the scent stays with me. "Bailey?" I say as I retrace my steps, hurry past her desk and into my office.

That's when I see the envelope.

It has my name on it in Bailey's familiar handwriting. I rip it open. The note inside is short and polite and to the point. She writes that today is the last day on which she can accept or reject a new position.

A new position?

She writes that she has decided she cannot turn down a new and exciting opportunity, and that she regrets not giving me longer notice, but it slipped her mind.

Slipped her mind? That steel-trap of a mind?

She assures me that all her work is up to date, and that she's taken the liberty of arranging for a temp to come in. She includes the temp's VC. I don't read it, but a bunch of letters—B.A., M.A.—damn near leap off the page. That's it. The entire note. Oh, except for the last bit.

Sincerely yours,
Bailey B. Abrams

I SINK INTO MY CHAIR. I read the note again. She's really done this. She's left me. She's gone.

Goddammit!

She's left me without notice. Without giving a crap for what effect this will have on the day-to-day operation of O'Malley Design and Construction. Exactly how long has she been contemplating this? Was she head-hunted? Did she go out looking for a new job? Did she know all this when we were away together this weekend? Yes. Obviously she did. So was she composing this note when we were in bed? When we were making love?

Shit.

I shoot to my feet and kick my chair. Ouch! Talk about stupid moves...

Yeah, but nothing as stupid as giving a fancy name to something as basic as good old-fashioned fucking. We fucked. Making love had nothing to do with it. Making love is female talk, a way of pretending lust isn't lust.

I tell myself to calm down.

Then I read the note again.

I must have misunderstood it the first time. I see what my PA wrote, but is it true? Maybe she left because she can't face me after what happened between us this weekend. She's naïve. She doesn't know how to handle the aftermath of a simple sexual encounter.

Of a what? a little voice inside me says, but I ignore it.

She doesn't know how to deal with what happened and now she's worried that we won't be able to continue our relationship in a businesslike manner, which is patently ridiculous. Yes, I was upset yesterday.

Yes, I couldn't get the images out of my mind. Bailey in my arms. Bailey opening her thighs to me. Bailey writhing in ecstasy as I suck her nipples and, dammit, Bailey sitting in that big bed with me, eating pizza and laughing and talking about everything and anything...

Now I'm more than angry. I'm totally pissed.

And it's all her fault. She was too embarrassed to see me again. Okay. I understand that. But to walk away and leave me in the lurch...

To walk away and leave me a note that never even hints at what we did this weekend, what we shared...

I kick the chair again, never mind the sharp pain that radiates through my foot.

"Who gives a crap about that?" I yell.

I guess I yell pretty loud because I hear a clearing of the throat in the silence that follows and when I turn around, I see a woman standing in the doorway to my office. I've never seen her before and from the look on her face, she's about to scurry away and make sure I never see her again. She's wearing a black suit and carrying a black briefcase and I know instantly she is the temp Bailey hired. Hey, I am nothing if not a brilliant observer.

"Sorry," she says. "I, ah, I should have waited..."

"No." I flash what I hope like hell is a smile. "Please. Come in." I hold out my hand. "I'm Matt O'Malley. And you're..." Her name escapes me. "The temp. With the B.A. and the M.A."

She nods. And shakes my hand. She even smiles. "Eleanor Griffith. Did I, um, did I show up too early? I can come by later, if you prefer."

I glance at my watch. It's five minutes before nine.

"No, this is fine. I'm just—I'm a little pressured this morning, that's all. Your predecessor's departure was kind of sudden."

"I know. She told me about that job offer, how her new employer insisted she show up in Minneapolis tomorrow the latest or—"

"Minneapolis?"

"Right." Eleanor Griffith looks around her. "I assume that desk just outside your door is mine."

"Right. Yes." I stare at her. "Are you sure she said Minneapolis?"

"Positive, sir." She pauses. "I'd like to get straight to work, Mr. O'Malley, if that's all right with—"

"That's impossible. She can't move out of the city."

My temp raises her eyebrows. "Well," she says cautiously, "I don't really know if she can or if she can't. I mean—"

"Leaving New York is not acceptable."

Eleanor Griffith takes a step back. "Is she—is she on probation? Because I once worked for a gentleman who, it turned out, was on—"

"I forbid it! I forbid her to move! And, Jesus H. Christ, to Minneapolis? Have you ever been there? Hot summers. Endless winters. Glassed-in walkways between buildings so you don't melt in the summer or turn into Frosty the Snowman in the winter as you go from one place to another."

The temp takes a couple of more steps back. "I believe they're called skyways, sir."

"Who cares what they're called? She won't have the

good sense to use them. She'll take the streets and she'll freeze to death. Or she'll turn into a puddle of sweat because she'll wear those hideous suits rather than let anyone see how beautiful she really is."

Eleanor Griffith spins on her heel and hurries away. "Cancel all my appointments," I yell after her, but she's turned the corner and she's gone.

The rest of my staff, however, is all here, standing at the end of the hall when I reach it, and they're staring at me.

"Matt?" one of them says.

It's Jack, my accountant. "Cancel my appointments," I bark.

Jack looks bewildered. "I don't even know where your calendar is."

I laugh, but from the hasty scrape of feet as everybody gets out of my way, it isn't a pretty sound.

"So what?" I say. "Neither do I."

Two minutes later, I'm in my car, burning rubber.

ONE OF THE good things about driving is that it always has a calming effect on me.

Okay, it takes a while for that to happen this morning, but by the time I reach the city, I am in much better shape. I've figured things out and now I can act accordingly.

For starters, forget that nonsense about Bailey moving to Minneapolis. She's a New Yorker to the bone. No way is she going to leave Manhattan.

Second, she's not embarrassed.

All right. Maybe she is. A little. But mostly she simply needs assurance that what happened over the weekend won't affect her career. And why would it? Fucking was a one-off. Well, maybe a three or four-off. Maybe, if I stop and count, a six-off. Actually, I have no idea how many times we made love—and, dammit, what does it matter if I say we fucked or we made love? The point is, I didn't keep track. I was too lost in Bailey, in holding her, being with her. In that big bed. In the soaking tub. Over the back of the chair in front of that little writing desk. In that enormous shower and yes, on that marble bench although that time I sat her on the bench, went down on my knees, spread her thighs wide...

Honk!

I push the wheel to the right and avoid the truck coming at me. It's the truck driver's fault. What's he doing, edging into my lane?

Okay.

I am not calm. Not yet. And I need to be calm if I'm going to make Bailey see what a huge mistake she's making, giving up her job as my PA. She has a career here. And I need her. She's a fantastic PA, the best a man could have. I'll miss her talent for organization, her ability to make a difficult day seem easy...

Dammit.

I'll miss her laugh. Her sense of humor. The way she stands up to me. And I never got around to teaching her anything substantive about football.

I am definitely not calm.

Deep breathing will do it. Mindfulness. Inhale. One. Two. Three. Four. Five. Hold. And exhale. One. Two Three…

I am fine by the time I get to Bailey's apartment building. I have a moment of panic when I spot the big truck parked in front of it. Is it a moving truck? No. It's just a delivery truck. Of course it isn't a moving truck. Bailey is not going anywhere, certainly not to Minneapolis.

There's no place to park. There probably isn't one for another twenty blocks. This is New York, remember? Not Minneapolis. Or Philadelphia. Or Boston. And yes, I know there aren't parking spaces in those cities either, but that isn't my point. My point is that my PA is from this town and she would never leave it.

That's what I tell myself as I pull into a bus stop and get out of my car. It's what I tell myself as I go to Bailey's building and ring a bell at random so that somebody will ring back and let me in.

It's what I tell myself as I go inside and take the steps two at a time.

It's even what I tell myself as I punch her doorbell.

I must be out of shape, otherwise why would my heart be beating so fast?

I'm about to ring the bell again when I hear the snick of the peephole being opened. For the first time in maybe the last hour, I can actually breathe. Not the one, two, three, four, five stuff. Just breathe, in and out, because now I know she's really still here.

I hear the peephole snick closed and I brace myself for what she's going to say when she opens the door.

I've thought about it in the car, coming here, and I know what it'll be. She'll tell me that we crossed a line by sleeping together over the weekend and I'll tell her that she's correct. We shouldn't have done it. We should have left our relationship strictly professional and what happened was all my fault and we are adults and the past is the past. I'll admit that not only don't I want to lose her as my PA, I don't want to lose her as my friend because she has become my friend in the last week. She always was my friend and I was too blind to see it.

I'm prepared to tell her all those things, but I can't because she doesn't open the door.

I ring the bell again.

Nothing.

I hit the bell with the heel of my hand.

Still nothing.

Stay calm, I tell myself...and I ball up my fist and pound on the door until it shudders.

"Bailey," I shout, "open this door!"

Two other doors creak open, but not hers. I glare at the other doors and since true New Yorkers are standing behind them, both doors quickly close. I turn my attention to the door that matters and bang on it again.

"Dammit, Bailey, I know you're in there..."

Locks click and jingle. The door opens. "Stop that," my PA hisses.

I shove the door open and march inside her apartment. Her cat stands in the middle of the room, back arched.

"Yeah," I tell the cat, "the exact same to you."

I look around the room and my calm gives way to fury. Why wouldn't it, when I see boxes stacked near the sofa?

"You are not," I say, as I elbow the door shut, "absolutely not moving to Minneapolis."

Bailey folds her arms over her chest. "I will move wherever I please, Mr. O'Malley."

"Do you even know about those skyways in Minneapolis?"

She wrinkles her forehead. "What are you talking about?"

"See? You don't know about them. How can you move to Minneapolis when you don't know they have skyways?"

"Mr. O'Malley..."

"It's Matthew."

"It should have stayed Mr. O'Malley. Now, if you don't mind—"

"How dare you quit your job?"

Her chin comes up. "How *dare* I?"

"What about your responsibilities to me?"

"I hired an excellent replacement."

"An excellent replacement!" I can feel the corner of my mouth curl. "The woman ran at the first little problem."

Bailey sighs. "Look, my only regret is that I didn't give you more notice. There just wasn't time."

"Is that really your only regret?"

Somehow, my rage has drained away. What I feel

instead is a kind of emptiness. I look at Bailey and I see that same emotion in her eyes.

Something knots deep inside me.

She is not dressed for work or for company. Her hair is hanging loose; she's wearing another slightly shrunken T-shirt. And yoga pants. This pair is old; there's a tiny hole in one leg. I can see a glimpse of her skin.

I can remember the feel of that skin. Its silky softness.

The knot inside me tightens.

"I'm sorry," I say softly.

She nods. Her eyes glitter. She swings away and rubs at them. "Yes. I am too."

"I only wanted to help," I say. "Instead, I totally screwed things up."

"It wasn't you. It was me. I should never have—"

I capture her shoulders with my hands and gently turn her towards me. "It was wrong. I was wrong. Not for making love to you." I reach out and catch a dark curl between my fingers. "For thinking we could keep it all a game."

She nods again. Her eyes are damp. I want to kiss away that dampness, but I know it would be a mistake. I have to tell her some things first. Important things. Things I've only just learned, but not here. Not with Priscilla glaring at us from her perch on the stack of boxes, not with the sounds of the city intruding.

"Bailey?"

She looks at me.

"We have to talk."

She shakes her head. I capture her chin in my hand.

"Okay," I say, "*I* have to talk. Will you come for a ride with me?"

"Matthew. I don't think that's a good idea."

She's back to calling me Matthew. I tell myself that's meaningful.

"Please," I say. "Come with me. And if you don't like what I have to tell you, I'll bring you back here and you can—you can go to Minneapolis."

At first, I think she's going to turn me down flat. Then she gives a sad little laugh. "Do you really think I'd leave New York?"

"The boxes?"

"Old clothes. For the Manhattan Shelters Clothing Drive." She manages a quick smile. "Somebody's going to be happy getting all those old suits."

I smile too. The knot inside me is still there, but at least it hasn't gotten any tighter.

"Come with me," I say.

I wait. And wait. Then my Bailey sighs, grabs a sweatshirt from the sofa, scratches Priscilla behind the ear, and we head out the door.

17

S he doesn't ask where we're going.

That's good, especially since I only just figured it out myself.

Wrong. I didn't figure it out. It just came to me, the one place, the one right place where I need to take her. It's almost an hour away and by the time I turn off the highway and I begin to navigate the series of country roads that lead to our destination, my palms are sweaty and my heart is pounding the same way it did a while ago when I stood outside Bailey's door.

I was the kid who thought nothing of facing down a defensive line of three hundred pound behemoths. The kid who took off for places that were only names on a map with a backpack and a bankcard. I turned into the guy who used to bet six figures on a stock without blinking, who walked away from all that so I could go into debt with little more than hope and a dream.

Yeah, but this is different.

I turn up a narrow dirt road that winds into a heavy stand of trees.

Bailey looks at me. "Where are we?" she asks, but as the trees open up just enough to reveal a gentle hill that overlooks a lake and an untouched valley, she catches her breath. "This is that property," she says. "The one you wouldn't put the wrong house on."

I pull the car under a tree, get out, go around to Bailey's side. She's sitting perfectly still and since I know she's not the kind of woman to wait for a man to open a door for her, it scares me that she's not moving.

I reach for the door, but she beats me to it, unlatches the door and steps from the car.

"I'm right, aren't I?" she says softly. "About this land?"

"Yes."

She starts up the slope beside me. There's a light breeze. It ruffles her hair.

It's as if the place has been waiting for her.

We reach the top. She catches her breath.

"Oh," she whispers, "It's beautiful."

I nod. It is beautiful. The land. The trees. The view. The sense of being alone on the planet.

Alone, but not lonely. Not anymore.

How come I never realized that? That I was lonely? That I would never know joyfulness until I found the missing half of my soul?

I take a deep breath and clasp Bailey's shoulders as she stands with her back to me.

"Bailey," I say. "there's no easy way to tell you this…"

She turns towards me. She's crying, and I reach out and brush the tears from her cheeks with my thumbs.

"It's all right," she says. "There's nothing to apologize for. What happened this weekend was—it was everything I'd ever dreamed. It's what I meant when I said I was the one who'd lied because—because I'd always wanted you, Matthew. I was a fool to let myself give in to worrying about what others would think. I have no regrets. Not one. I want you to know that, but I can't keep working with you. It's too much, too much, too much—"

There's only one way to silence her and I take it.

I cup her face. I capture her lips. I kiss her with everything I am, everything I hope to be.

I kiss her with all the love in my heart.

"I love you," I say against her mouth. "I've loved you for years. I've loved you forever." She stares at me. "Bailey? Did you hear what I said? I love—"

She says my name. And, hell, she's crying even harder than she was a couple of seconds ago.

"Honey," I say, "please, doesn't cry. I never meant to make you cry."

"Matthew." She rises on her toes and clasps my face. "Matthew, say it again."

"Say what again? That I love you?"

"Yes," she says, and now she's laughing and crying at the same time. "Tell me that you love me, because I love you with all my heart."

I take a deep breath. "Bailey. Sweetheart. Will you marry me?"

Another woman might drag out the moment. Give

her man a little punishment. But this isn't another woman, this is *my* woman. My PA.

My Bailey.

"Yes," she says, "yes, yes, yes!"

So, yeah, what I told you at the beginning was true.

This is a romance, my beautiful wife's and mine.

We marry on a beautiful fall afternoon.

We have the ceremony right here, on our hilltop. We've already begun putting up our house, a sprawling contemporary that will blend into the land and the woods and, we hope, not disturb the creatures who also call this land home.

Bailey asks Casey to be her matron of honor. Coop is my best man. My little niece toddles down the aisle first, tossing flower petals in all directions.

We have a small wedding, because that's how we both want it. Only people who matter share the day with us. There's no ostentation, no glitter, no big buffet. Instead, my guys have put up a party tent and Casey's come up with a caterer who's done amazing things with free range chicken, grass-fed beef, tofu and tempeh. I have the feeling I can see all-out vegetarianism in my future, but that's all right.

As long as Bailey and I have each other, we'll be fine.

After the ceremony, after the party, when we are finally alone, we linger on our hillside, standing wrapped in each other's arms as we try to count the stars.

"Impossible to do," I say.

Bailey turns to me and smiles. And I am again reminded that it *is* possible to count the stars, the ones in my wife's eyes.

"I have a confession to make," she says softly.

I link my hands at the base of her spine. "Yeah?"

"Didn't you ever wonder how come I just happened to be on the pill that weekend we went to my cousin's wedding?"

Actually, I had wondered, but I knew some women took the pill to regulate their periods, or maybe just to be prepared.

I smile and drop a kiss on my wife's hair. "Okay. How come?"

Her lips curve in an answering smile. "I went to my doctor's office in the morning. Before we left. And I asked him for a prescription."

"Oh." And then it hits me. "You mean—"

"I mean," she says, "I was determined to have my way with you that weekend, Mr. O'Malley, whether you were ready or not."

I laugh softly. "Mrs. O'Malley, you are a wicked woman."

My wife rises on her toes and brings her mouth to mine. "And you like me that way," she whispers.

"I *love* you that way," I tell her. "I love you all the ways you are."

She sighs and clasps my face between her hands.

"I love you, Matthew," she says. "I adore you."

"That's good," I say. "Because I would be lost if you didn't." I lean my forehead against hers. "I will love you forever, sweetheart."

Bailey smiles. "Forever,."

And just in case you're reading this and you still don't get my message, here it is.

If you're lucky, really lucky, Forever is the only F-Word that counts.

END

www.sandramarton.com

AFTERWORD

Sandra Marton, a USA Today Bestselling Author, is a four-time Rita finalist, a member of RWA's Honor Roll, and a proud recipient of RWA's Centennial Award. You can find out more about her books at her website www.sandramarton.com, and at Amazon, iBooks, Barnes & Noble, Kobo, and Google Play.